I want to give a really *bad* party. I mean it. I want to give a party where there's a brawl and seductions and people going home with their feelings hurt and women passed out in the *cabinet de toilette*. You wait and see.

1 3 5 7 9 10 8 6 4 2

Vintage
20 Vauxhall Bridge Road,
London SW1V 2SA

Vintage Classics is part of the Penguin Random House group of companies whose addresses can be found at global.penguinrandomhouse.com

Penguin
Random House
UK

The Great Gatsby was first published in 1925, *Tender is the Night* was first published in 1934, 'Bernice Bobs her Hair', 'The Bridal Party' and 'The Baby Party' from *The Collected Short Stories* first published in 1986.

This edition published by Vintage in 2020

penguin.co.uk/vintage

A CIP catalogue record for this book is available from the British Library

ISBN 9781784876067

Typeset in 10.5/14.5 pt FreightText Pro
by Jouve (UK), Milton Keynes
Printed and bound in Great Britain by Clays Ltd, Elcograf S.p.A.

Parties

F. SCOTT FITZGERALD

VINTAGE MINIS

Contents

1

The Great Gatsby

THERE WAS MUSIC from my neighbour's house through the summer nights. In his blue gardens men and girls came and went like moths among the whisperings and the champagne and the stars. At high tide in the afternoon I watched his guests diving from the tower of his raft, or taking the sun on the hot sand of his beach while his two motor-boats slit the waters of the Sound, drawing aquaplanes over cataracts of foam. On week-ends his Rolls-Royce became an omnibus, bearing parties to and from the city between nine in the morning and long past midnight, while his station wagon scampered like a brisk yellow bug to meet all trains. And on Mondays eight servants, including an extra gardener, toiled all day with mops and scrubbing-brushes and hammers and garden-shears, repairing the ravages of the night before.

Every Friday five crates of oranges and lemons arrived from a fruiterer in New York – every Monday these same oranges and lemons left his back door in a pyramid of pulpless halves. There was a machine in the kitchen which could extract the juice of two hundred oranges in half an hour if a little button was pressed two hundred times by a butler's thumb.

At least once a fortnight a corps of caterers came down with several hundred feet of canvas and enough coloured lights to make a Christmas tree of Gatsby's enormous garden. On buffet tables, garnished with glistening hors d'œuvre, spiced baked hams crowded against salads of harlequin designs and pastry pigs and turkeys bewitched to a dark gold. In the main hall a bar with a real brass rail was set up, and stocked with gins and liquors and with cordials so long forgotton that most of his female guests were too young to know one from another.

By seven o'clock the orchestra has arrived, no thin five-piece affair, but a whole pitful of oboes and trombones and saxophones and viols and cornets and piccolos, and low and high drums. The last swimmers have come in from the beach now and are dressing upstairs; the cars from New York are parked five deep in the drive, and already the halls and salons and verandas are gaudy with primary colours, and hair bobbed in strange new ways, and shawls beyond the dreams of Castile. The bar is in full swing, and floating rounds of cocktails permeate the garden outside, until the air is alive with chatter and laughter, and casual innuendo and introductions forgotten on the spot, and enthusiastic meetings between women who never knew each other's names.

The lights grow brighter as the earth lurches away from the sun, and now the orchestra is playing yellow cocktail music, and the opera of voices pitches a key higher. Laughter is easier minute by minute, spilled with prodigality, tipped out at a cheerful word. The groups change more swiftly, swell with new arrivals, dissolve and form in the same breath; already there are wanderers, confident girls who weave here and there among the stouter and more stable, become for a sharp, joyous moment the centre of a group, and then, excited with triumph, glide on through the sea-change of faces and voices and colour under the constantly changing light.

Suddenly one of these gypsies, in trembling opal, seizes a cocktail out of the air, dumps it down for courage and, moving her hands like Frisco, dances out alone on the canvas platform. A momentary hush; the orchestra leader varies his rhythm obligingly for her, and there is a burst of chatter as the erroneous news goes around that she is Gilda Gray's understudy from the *Follies*. The party has begun.

I believe that on the first night I went to Gatsby's house I was one of the few guests who had actually been invited. People were not invited – they went there. They got into automobiles which bore them out to Long Island, and somehow they ended up at Gatsby's door. Once there they were introduced by somebody who knew Gatsby, and after that they conducted themselves according to the rules of behaviour associated with an amusement park. Sometimes they came and went without having met Gatsby at all, came for the party with a simplicity of heart that was its own ticket of admission.

I had been actually invited. A chauffeur in a uniform of robin's-egg blue crossed my lawn early that Saturday morning with a surprisingly formal note from his employer: the honour would be entirely Gatsby's, it said, if I would attend his 'little party' that night. He had seen me several times, and had intended to call on me long before, but a peculiar combination of circumstances had prevented it – signed Jay Gatsby, in a majestic hand.

Dressed up in white flannels I went over to his lawn a little while after seven, and wandered around rather ill at ease among swirls and eddies of people I didn't know – though here and there was a face I had noticed on the commuting train. I was immediately struck by the number of young Englishmen dotted about; all well dressed, all looking a little hungry, and all talking in low, earnest voices to solid and prosperous Americans. I was sure that they were selling something: bonds or insurance or automobiles. They were at least agonizingly aware of the easy money in the vicinity and convinced that it was theirs for a few words in the right key.

As soon as I arrived I made an attempt to find my host, but the two or three people of whom I asked his whereabouts stared at me in such an amazed way, and denied so vehemently any knowledge of his movements, that I slunk off in the direction of the cocktail table – the only place in the garden where a single man could linger without looking purposeless and alone.

I was on my way to get roaring drunk from sheer embarrassment when Jordan Baker came out of the house and stood at the head of the marble steps, leaning a little backward and looking with contemptuous interest down into the garden.

Welcome or not, I found it necessary to attach myself to someone before I should begin to address cordial remarks to the passers-by.

'Hello!' I roared, advancing towards her. My voice seemed unnaturally loud across the garden.

'I thought you might be here,' she responded absently as I came up. 'I remembered you lived next door to—'

She held my hand impersonally, as a promise that she'd take care of me in a minute, and gave ear to two girls in twin yellow dresses, who stopped at the foot of the steps.

'Hello!' they cried together. 'Sorry you didn't win.'

That was for the golf tournament. She had lost in the finals the week before.

'You don't know who we are,' said one of the girls in yellow, 'but we met you here about a month ago.'

'You've dyed your hair since then,' remarked Jordan, and I started, but the girls had moved casually on and her remark was addressed to the premature moon, produced like the supper, no doubt, out of a caterer's basket. With Jordan's slender golden arm resting in mine, we descended the steps and sauntered about the garden. A tray of cocktails floated at us through the twilight, and we sat down at a table with the two girls in yellow and three men, each one introduced to us as Mr Mumble.

'Do you come to these parties often?' inquired Jordan of the girl beside her.

'The last one was the one I met you at,' answered the girl, in an alert confident voice. She turned to her companion: 'Wasn't it for you, Lucille?'

It was for Lucille, too.

'I like to come,' Lucille said. 'I never care what I do, so I always have a good time. When I was here last I tore my gown on a chair, and he asked me my name and address – inside of a week I got a package from Croirier's with a new evening gown in it.'

'Did you keep it?' asked Jordan.

'Sure I did. I was going to wear it tonight, but it

was too big in the bust and had to be altered. It was gas blue and lavender beads. Two hundred and sixty-five dollars.'

'There's something funny about a fellow that'll do a thing like that,' said the other girl eagerly. 'He doesn't want any trouble with *any*body.'

'Who doesn't?' I inquired.

'Gatsby. Somebody told me—'

The two girls and Jordan leaned together confidentially.

'Somebody told me they thought he killed a man once.'

A thrill passed over all of us. The three Mr Mumbles bent forward and listened eagerly.

'I don't think it's so much *that*,' argued Lucille sceptically; 'it's more that he was a German spy during the war.'

One of the men nodded in confirmation.

'I heard that from a man who knew all about him, grew up with him in Germany,' he assured us positively.

'Oh, no,' said the first girl, 'it couldn't be that, because he was in the American army during the war.' As our credulity switched back to her she leaned forward with enthusiasm. 'You look at him sometimes when he thinks nobody's looking at him. I'll bet he killed a man.'

She narrowed her eyes and shivered. Lucille

shivered. We all turned and looked around for Gatsby. It was testimony to the romantic speculation he inspired that there were whispers about him from those who had found little that it was necessary to whisper about in this world.

The first supper – there would be another one after midnight – was now being served, and Jordan invited me to join her own party, who were spread around a table on the other side of the garden. There were three married couples and Jordan's escort, a persistent undergraduate given to violent innuendo, and obviously under the impression that sooner or later Jordan was going to yield him up her person to a greater or lesser degree. Instead of rambling, this party had preserved a dignified homogeneity, and assumed to itself the function of representing the staid nobility of the countryside – East Egg condescending to West Egg, and carefully on guard against its spectroscopic gaiety.

'Let's get out,' whispered Jordan, after a somehow wasteful and inappropriate half-hour; 'this is much too polite for me.'

We got up, and she explained that we were going to find the host: I had never met him, she said, and it was making me uneasy. The undergraduate nodded in a cynical, melancholy way.

The bar, where we glanced first, was crowded, but Gatsby was not there. She couldn't find him from the top of the steps, and he wasn't on the veranda. On a chance we tried an important-looking door, and walked into a high Gothic library, panelled with carved English oak, and probably transported complete from some ruin overseas.

A stout, middle-aged man, with enormous owl-eyed spectacles, was sitting somewhat drunk on the edge of a great table, staring with unsteady concentration at the shelves of books. As we entered he wheeled excitedly around and examined Jordan from head to foot.

'What do you think?' he demanded impetuously.

'About what?'

He waved his hand towards the book-shelves.

'About that. As a matter of fact you needn't bother to ascertain. I ascertained. They're real.'

'The books?'

He nodded.

'Absolutely real – have pages and everything. I thought they'd be a nice durable cardboard. Matter of fact, they're absolutely real. Pages and – Here! Lemme show you.'

Taking our scepticism for granted, he rushed to the bookcases and returned with Volume One of the 'Stoddard Lectures.'

'See!' he cried triumphantly. 'It's a bona-fide piece of printed matter. It fooled me. This fella's a regular Belasco. It's a triumph. What thoroughness! What realism! Knew when to stop, too – didn't cut the pages. But what do you want? What do you expect?'

He snatched the book from me and replaced it hastily on its shelf, muttering that if one brick was removed the whole library was liable to collapse.

'Who brought you?' he demanded. 'Or did you just come? I was brought. Most people were brought.'

Jordan looked at him alertly, cheerfully, without answering.

'I was brought by a woman named Roosevelt,' he continued. 'Mrs Claude Roosevelt. Do you know her? I met her somewhere last night. I've been drunk for about a week now, and I thought it might sober me up to sit in a library.'

'Has it?'

'A little bit, I think. I can't tell yet. I've only been here an hour. Did I tell you about the books? They're real. They're—'

'You told us.'

We shook hands with him gravely and went back outdoors.

There was dancing now on the canvas in the garden; old men pushing young girls backwards in eternal graceless circles, superior couples holding each other tortuously, fashionably, and keeping in the corners – and a great number of single girls dancing individualistically or relieving the orchestra for a moment of the burden of the banjo or the traps. By midnight the hilarity had increased. A celebrated tenor had sung in Italian, and a notorious contralto had sung in jazz, and between the numbers people were doing 'stunts' all over the garden, while happy, vacuous bursts of laughter rose towards the summer sky. A pair of stage twins, who turned out to be the girls in yellow, did a baby act in costume, and champagne was served in glasses bigger than finger-bowls. The moon had risen higher, and floating in the Sound was a triangle of silver scales, trembling a little to the stiff, tinny drip of the banjoes on the lawn.

I was still with Jordan Baker. We were sitting at a table with a man of about my age and a rowdy little girl, who gave way upon the slightest provocation to uncontrollable laughter. I was enjoying myself now. I had taken two finger-bowls of champagne, and the scene had changed before my eyes into something significant, elemental, and profound.

At a lull in the entertainment the man looked at me and smiled.

'Your face is familiar,' he said, politely. 'Weren't you in the First Division during the war?'

'Why, yes. I was in the Twenty-eighth Infantry.'

'I was in the Sixteenth until June nineteen-eighteen. I knew I'd seen you somewhere before.'

We talked for a moment about some wet, grey little villages in France. Evidently he lived in this vicinity, for he told me that he had just bought a hydroplane, and was going to try it out in the morning.

'Want to go with me, old sport? Just near the shore along the Sound.'

'What time?'

'Any time that suits you best.'

It was on the tip of my tongue to ask his name when Jordan looked around and smiled.

'Having a gay time now?' she inquired.

'Much better.' I turned again to my new acquaintance. 'This is an unusual party for me. I haven't even seen the host. I live over there –' I waved my hand at the invisible hedge in the distance, 'and this man Gatsby sent over his chauffeur with an invitation.'

For a moment he looked at me as if he failed to understand.

'I'm Gatsby,' he said suddenly.

'What!' I exclaimed. 'Oh, I beg your pardon.'

'I thought you knew, old sport. I'm afraid I'm not a very good host.'

He smiled understandingly – much more than understandingly. It was one of those rare smiles with a quality of eternal reassurance in it, that you may come across four or five times in life. It faced – or seemed to face – the whole eternal world for an instant, and then concentrated on you with an irresistible prejudice in your favour. It understood you just as far as you wanted to be understood, believed in you as you would like to believe in yourself, and assured you that it had precisely the impression of you that, at your best, you hoped to convey. Precisely at that point it vanished – and I was looking at an elegant young roughneck, a year or two over thirty, whose elaborate formality of speech just missed being absurd. Some time before he introduced himself I'd got a strong impression that he was picking his words with care.

Almost at the moment when Mr Gatsby identified himself, a butler hurried towards him with the information that Chicago was calling him on the wire. He excused himself with a small bow that included each of us in turn.

'If you want anything just ask for it, old sport,' he urged me. 'Excuse me. I will rejoin you later.'

When he was gone I turned immediately to Jordan – constrained to assure her of my surprise. I had expected that Mr Gatsby would be a florid and corpulent person in his middle years.

'Who is he?' I demanded. 'Do you know?'

'He's just a man named Gatsby.'

'Where is he from, I mean? And what does he do?'

'Now *you're* started on the subject,' she answered with a wan smile. 'Well, he told me once he was an Oxford man.'

A dim background started to take shape behind him, but at her next remark it faded away.

'However, I don't believe it.'

'Why not?'

'I don't know,' she insisted, 'I just don't think he went there.'

Something in her tone reminded me of the other girl's 'I think he killed a man,' and had the effect of stimulating my curiosity. I would have accepted without question the information that Gatsby sprang from the swamps of Louisiana or from the lower East Side of New York. That was comprehensible. But young men didn't – at least in my provincial inexperience I believed they didn't – drift coolly out of nowhere and buy a palace on Long Island Sound.

'Anyhow, he gives large parties,' said Jordan, changing the subject with an urban taste for the concrete. 'And I like large parties. They're so intimate. At small parties there isn't any privacy.'

There was the boom of a brass drum, and the voice of the orchestra leader rang out suddenly above the echolalia of the garden.

'Ladies and gentlemen,' he cried. 'At the request of Mr Gatsby we are going to play for you Mr Vladimir Tostoff's latest work, which attracted so much attention at Carnegie Hall last May. If you read the papers, you know there was a big sensation.' He smiled with jovial condescension, and added: 'Some sensation!' Whereupon everybody laughed.

'The piece is known,' he concluded lustily, 'as Vladimir Tostoff's *Jazz History of the World.*'

The nature of Mr Tostoff's composition eluded me, because just as it began my eyes fell on Gatsby, standing alone on the marble steps and looking from one group to another with approving eyes. His tanned skin was drawn attractively tight on his face and his short hair looked as though it were trimmed every day. I could see nothing sinister about him. I wondered if the fact that he was not drinking helped to set him off from his guests, for it seemed to me that he grew more correct as the fraternal hilarity increased. When the *Jazz History of the World* was over, girls were putting their heads on men's shoulders in a puppyish, convivial way, girls were swooning backward playfully into men's arms, even into groups, knowing that someone would arrest their falls – but no one swooned backward on Gatsby, and no French bob touched Gatsby's shoulder, and no singing quartets were formed with Gatsby's head for one link.

'I beg your pardon.'

Gatsby's butler was suddenly standing beside us.

'Miss Baker?' he inquired. 'I beg your pardon, but Mr Gatsby would like to speak to you alone.'

'With me?' she exclaimed in surprise.

'Yes, madame.'

She got up slowly, raising her eyebrows at me in astonishment, and followed the butler towards the house. I noticed that she wore her evening-dress, all her dresses, like sports clothes – there was a jauntiness about her movements as if she had first learned to walk upon golf courses on clean, crisp mornings.

I was alone and it was almost two. For some time confused and intriguing sounds had issued from a long, many-windowed room which overhung the terrace. Eluding Jordan's undergraduate, who was now engaged in an obstetrical conversation with two chorus girls, and who implored me to join him, I went inside.

The large room was full of people. One of the girls in yellow was playing the piano, and beside her stood a tall, red-haired young lady from a famous chorus, engaged in song. She had drunk a quantity of champagne, and during the course of her song she had decided, ineptly, that everything was very, very sad – she was not only singing, she was weeping too. Whenever there was a pause in the song she filled it with gasping, broken sobs, and then took up the lyric again in a quavering soprano. The tears coursed down her cheeks – not freely, however, for when they came into contact with her heavily beaded eyelashes they assumed an inky colour, and pursued the rest of their way in slow black rivulets. A humorous suggestion was made that she sing the notes on her face, whereupon she threw up her hands, sank into a chair, and went off into a deep vinous sleep.

'She had a fight with a man who says he's her husband,' explained a girl at my elbow.

I looked around. Most of the remaining women were now having fights with men said to be their husbands. Even Jordan's party, the quartet from East Egg, were rent asunder by dissension. One of the men was talking with curious intensity to a young actress, and his wife, after attempting to laugh at the situation in a dignified and indifferent way, broke down entirely and resorted to flank attacks – at intervals she appeared suddenly at his side like an angry diamond, and hissed: 'You promised!' into his ear.

The reluctance to go home was not confined to wayward men. The hall was at present occupied by two deplorably sober men and their highly indignant wives. The wives were sympathizing with each other in slightly raised voices.

'Whenever he sees I'm having a good time he wants to go home.'

'Never heard anything so selfish in my life.'

'We're always the first ones to leave.'

'So are we.'

'Well, we're almost the last tonight,' said one of the men sheepishly. 'The orchestra left half an hour ago.'

In spite of the wives' agreement that such malevolence was beyond credibility, the dispute ended in a short struggle, and both wives were lifted, kicking, into the night.

As I waited for my hat in the hall the door of the library opened and Jordan Baker and Gatsby came out together. He was saying some last word to her, but the eagerness in his manner tightened abruptly into formality as several people approached him to say good-bye.

Jordan's party were calling impatiently to her from the porch, but she lingered for a moment to shake hands.

'I've just heard the most amazing thing,' she whispered. 'How long were we in there?'

'Why, about an hour.'

'It was . . . simply amazing,' she repeated abstractedly. 'But I swore I wouldn't tell it and here I am tantalizing you.' She yawned gracefully in my face. 'Please come and see me . . . Phone book . . . Under the name of Mrs Sigourney Howard . . . My aunt . . .' She was hurrying off as she talked – her brown hand waved a jaunty salute as she melted into her party at the door.

Rather ashamed that on my first appearance I had stayed so late, I joined the last of Gatsby's guests, who were clustered around him. I wanted to explain that I'd hunted for him early in the evening and to apologize for not having known him in the garden.

'Don't mention it,' he enjoined me eagerly. 'Don't give it another thought, old sport.' The familiar expression held no more familiarity than the hand which reassuringly brushed my shoulder. 'And don't forget we're going up in the hydroplane tomorrow morning, at nine o'clock.'

Then the butler, behind his shoulder:

'Philadelphia wants you on the 'phone, sir.'

'All right, in a minute. Tell them I'll be right there . . . Good night.'

'Good night.'

'Good night.' He smiled – and suddenly there seemed to be a pleasant significance in having been among the last to go, as if he had desired it all the time. 'Good night, old sport . . . Good night.'

But as I walked down the steps I saw that the evening was not quite over. Fifty feet from the door a dozen headlights illuminated a bizarre and tumultuous scene. In the ditch beside the road, right side up, but violently shorn of one wheel, rested a new coupé which had left Gatsby's drive not two minutes before. The sharp jut of a wall accounted for the detachment of the wheel, which was now getting considerable attention from half a dozen curious chauffeurs. However, as they had left their cars blocking the road, a harsh, discordant din from those in the rear had been audible for some time, and added to the already violent confusion of the scene.

A man in a long duster had dismounted from the wreck and now stood in the middle of the road, looking from the car to the tyre and from the tyre to the observers in a pleasant, puzzled way.

'See!' he explained. 'It went in the ditch.'

The fact was infinitely astonishing to him, and I recognized first the unusual quality of wonder, and then the man – it was the late patron of Gatsby's library.

'How'd it happen?'

He shrugged his shoulders.

'I know nothing whatever about mechanics,' he said decisively.

'But how did it happen? Did you run into the wall?'

'Don't ask me,' said Owl Eyes, washing his hands of the whole matter. 'I know very little about driving – next to nothing. It happened, and that's all I know.'

'Well, if you're a poor driver you oughtn't to try driving at night.'

'But I wasn't even trying,' he explained indignantly, 'I wasn't even trying.'

An awed hush fell upon the bystanders.

'Do you want to commit suicide?'

'You're lucky it was just a wheel! A bad driver and not even *try*ing!'

'You don't understand,' explained the criminal. 'I wasn't driving. There's another man in the car.'

The shock that followed this declaration found voice in a sustained 'Ah-h-h!' as the door of the coupé swung slowly open. The crowd – it was now a crowd – stepped back involuntarily, and when the door had opened wide there was a ghostly pause. Then, very gradually, part by part, a pale, dangling individual stepped out of the wreck, pawing tentatively at the ground with a large uncertain dancing shoe.

Blinded by the glare of the headlights and confused by the incessant groaning of the horns, the apparition stood swaying for a moment before he perceived the man in the duster.

'Wha's matter?' he inquired calmly. 'Did we run outa gas?'

'Look!'

Half a dozen fingers pointed at the amputated wheel – he stared at it for a moment, and then looked upward as though he suspected that it had dropped from the sky.

'It came off,' someone explained.

He nodded.

'At first I din' notice we'd stopped.'

A pause. Then, taking a long breath and straightening his shoulders, he remarked in a determined voice:

'Wonder'ff tell me where there's a gas'line station?'

At least a dozen men, some of them a little better off than he was, explained to him that wheel and car were no longer joined by any physical bond.

'Back out,' he suggested after a moment. 'Put her in reverse.'

'But the *wheel's* off!'

He hesitated.

'No harm in trying,' he said.

The caterwauling horns had reached a crescendo and I turned away and cut across the lawn towards home. I glanced back once. A wafer of a moon was shining over Gatsby's house, making the night fine as before, and surviving the laughter and the sound of his still glowing garden. A sudden emptiness seemed to flow now from the windows and the great doors, endowing with complete isolation the figure of the host, who stood on the porch, his hand up in a formal gesture of farewell.

2

Tender is the Night

I

FEELING GOOD FROM the rosy wine at lunch, Nicole Diver folded her arms high enough for the artificial camellia on her shoulder to touch her cheek, and went out into her lovely grassless garden. The garden was bounded on one side by the house, from which it flowed and into which it ran, on two sides by the old village, and on the last by the cliff falling by ledges to the sea.

Along the walls on the village side all was dusty, the wriggling vines, the lemon and eucalyptus trees, the casual wheel-barrow, left only a moment since, but already grown into the path, atrophied and faintly rotten. Nicole was invariably somewhat surprised that by turning in the other direction past a bed of peonies she walked into an area so green and cool that the leaves and petals were curled with tender damp.

Knotted at her throat she wore a lilac scarf that even in the achromatic sunshine cast its colour up to her face and down around her moving feet in a lilac shadow. Her face was hard, almost stern, save for the soft gleam of piteous doubt that looked from her green eyes. Her once fair hair had darkened, but she was lovelier now at twenty-four than she had been at eighteen, when her hair was brighter than she.

Following a walk marked by an intangible mist of bloom that followed the white border stones she came to a space overlooking the sea where there were lanterns asleep in the fig trees and a big table and wicker chairs and a great market umbrella from Sienna, all gathered about an enormous pine, the biggest tree in the garden. She paused there a moment, looking absently at a growth of nasturtiums and iris tangled at its foot, as though sprung from a careless handful of seeds, listening to the plaints and accusations of some nursery squabble in the house. When this died away on the summer air, she walked on, between kaleidoscopic peonies massed in pink clouds, black and brown tulips and fragile mauve-stemmed roses, transparent like sugar flowers in a confectioner's window – until, as if the scherzo of colour could reach no further intensity, it broke off suddenly in mid-air, and moist steps went down to a level five feet below.

Here there was a well with the boarding around it dank and slippery even on the brightest days. She went up the stairs on the other side and into the vegetable garden; she walked rather quickly; she liked to be active, though at times she gave an impression of repose that was at once static and evocative. This was because she knew few words and believed in none, and in the world she was rather silent, contributing just her share of urbane humour with a precision that approached meagreness. But at the moment when strangers tended to grow uncomfortable in the presence of this economy she would seize the topic and rush off with it, feverishly surprised with herself – then bring it back and relinquish it abruptly, almost timidly, like an obedient retriever, having been adequate and something more.

As she stood in the fuzzy green light of the vegetable garden, Dick crossed the path ahead of her going to his work house. Nicole waited silently till he had passed; then she went on through lines of prospective salads to a little menagerie where pigeons and rabbits and a parrot made a medley of insolent noises at her. Descending to another ledge she reached a low, curved wall and looked down seven hundred feet to the Mediterranean Sea.

She stood in the ancient hill village of Tarmes. The villa and its grounds were made out of a row of peasant dwellings that abutted on the cliff – five small houses had been combined to make the house and four destroyed to make the garden. The exterior walls were untouched so that from the road far below it was indistinguishable from the violet grey mass of the town.

For a moment Nicole stood looking down at the Mediterranean but there was nothing to do with that, even with her tireless hands. Presently Dick came out of his one-room house carrying a telescope and looked east toward Cannes. In a moment Nicole swam into his field of vision, whereupon he disappeared into his house and came out with a megaphone. He had many light mechanical devices.

'Nicole,' he shouted, 'I forgot to tell you that as a final apostolic gesture I invited Mrs Abrams, the woman with the white hair.'

'I suspected it. It's an outrage.'

The ease with which her reply reached him seemed to belittle his megaphone, so she raised her voice and called, 'Can you hear me?'

'Yes.' He lowered the megaphone and then raised it stubbornly. 'I'm going to invite some more people too. I'm going to invite the two young men.'

'All right,' she agreed placidly.

'I want to give a really *bad* party. I mean it. I want

to give a party where there's a brawl and seductions and people going home with their feelings hurt and women passed out in the *cabinet de toilette*. You wait and see.'

He went back into his house and Nicole saw that one of his most characteristic moods was upon him, the excitement that swept everyone up into it and was inevitably followed by his own form of melancholy, which he never displayed but at which she guessed. This excitement about things reached an intensity out of proportion to their importance, generating a really extraordinary virtuosity with people. Save among a few of the tough-minded and perennially suspicious, he had the power of arousing a fascinated and uncritical love. The reaction came when he realized the waste and extravagance involved. He sometimes looked back with awe at the carnivals of affection he had given, as a general might gaze upon a massacre he had ordered to satisfy an impersonal blood-lust.

But to be included in Dick Diver's world for a while was a remarkable experience: people believed he made special reservations about them, recognizing the proud uniqueness of their destinies, buried under the compromises of how many years. He won everyone quickly with an exquisite consideration and a politeness that moved so fast and intuitively that it could be examined only in its effect. Then, without caution, lest the first bloom of the relation wither, he opened the gate to his amusing world. So long as they subscribed to it completely, their happiness was his preoccupation, but at the first flicker of doubt as to its all-inclusiveness he evaporated before their eyes, leaving little communicable memory of what he had said or done.

At eight-thirty that evening he came out to meet his first guests, his coat carried rather ceremoniously, rather promisingly, in his hand, like a toreador's cape. It was characteristic that after greeting Rosemary and her mother he waited for them to speak first, as if to allow them the reassurance of their own voices in the new surroundings.

To resume Rosemary's point of view it should be said that, under the spell of the climb to Tarmes and the fresher air, she and her mother looked about appreciatively. Just as the personal qualities of extraordinary people can make themselves plain in an unaccustomed change of expression, so the intensely calculated perfection of Villa Diana transpired all at once through such minute failures as the chance apparition of a maid in the background or the perversity of a cook. While the first guests arrived bringing with them the excitement of the night, the domestic activity of the day receded past them gently, symbolized by the Diver children and their governess still at supper on the terrace.

'What a beautiful garden!' Mrs Speers exclaimed.

'Nicole's garden,' said Dick. 'She won't let it alone – she nags it all the time, worries about its diseases. Any day now I expect to have her come down with Powdery Mildew or Fly Speck, or Late Blight.' He pointed his forefinger decisively at Rosemary, saying with a lightness seeming to conceal a paternal interest, 'I'm going to save your reason – I'm going to give you a hat to wear on the beach.'

He turned them from the garden to the terrace, where he poured a cocktail. Earl Brady arrived, discovering Rosemary with surprise. His manner was softer than at the studio, as if his differentness had been put on at the gate, and Rosemary, comparing him instantly with Dick Diver, swung sharply toward the latter. In comparison Earl Brady seemed faintly gross, faintly ill-bred; once more, though, she felt an electric response to his person.

He spoke familiarly to the children, who were getting up from their outdoor supper.

'Hello, Lanier, how about a song? Will you and Topsy sing me a song?'

'What shall we sing?' agreed the little boy, with the odd chanting accent of American children brought up in France.

'That song about "*Mon ami Pierrot*".'

Brother and sister stood side by side without

self-consciousness and their voices soared sweet and shrill upon the evening air.

'Au clair de la lune
Mon ami Pierrot
Prête-moi ta plume
Pour écrire un mot
Ma chandelle est morte
Je n'ai plus de feu
Ouvre-moi ta porte
Pour l'amour de Dieu.'

The singing ceased and the children, their faces aglow with the late sunshine, stood smiling calmly at their success. Rosemary was thinking that the Villa Diana was the centre of the world. On such a stage some memorable thing was sure to happen. She lighted up higher as the gate tinkled open and the rest of the guests arrived in a body – the McKiscos, Mrs Abrams, Mr Dumphry, and Mr Campion came up to the terrace.

Rosemary had a sharp feeling of disappointment – she looked quickly at Dick, as though to ask an explanation of this incongruous mingling. But there was nothing unusual in his expression. He greeted his new guests with a proud bearing and an obvious deference to their infinite and unknown possibilities. She believed in him so much that presently she accepted the rightness of the McKiscos' presence as if she had expected to meet them all along.

'I've met you in Paris,' McKisco said to Abe North, who with his wife had arrived on their heels, 'in fact I've met you twice.'

'Yes, I remember,' Abe said.

'Then where was it?' demanded McKisco, not content to let well enough alone.

'Why, I think –' Abe got tired of the game, 'I can't remember.'

The interchange filled a pause and Rosemary's instinct was that something tactful should be said by somebody, but Dick made no attempt to break up the grouping formed by these late arrivals, not even to disarm Mrs McKisco of her air of supercilious amusement. He did not solve this social problem because he knew it was not of importance at the moment and would solve itself. He was saving his newness for a larger effort, waiting a more significant moment for his guests to be conscious of a good time.

Rosemary stood beside Tommy Barban – he was in a particularly scornful mood and there seemed to be some special stimulus working upon him. He was leaving in the morning.

'Going home?'

'Home? I have no home. I am going to a war.'

'What war?'

'What war? Any war. I haven't seen a paper lately but I suppose there's a war – there always is.'

'Don't you care what you fight for?'

'Not at all – so long as I'm well treated. When I'm in a rut I come to see the Divers, because then I know that in a few weeks I'll want to go to war.'

Rosemary stiffened.

'You like the Divers,' she reminded him.

'Of course – especially her – but they make me want to go to war.'

She considered this, to no avail. The Divers made her want to stay near them for ever.

'You're half American,' she said, as if that should solve the problem.

'Also I'm half French, and I was educated in England and since I was eighteen I've worn the uniforms of eight countries. But I hope I did not give you the impression that I am not fond of the Divers – I am, especially of Nicole.'

'How could anyone help it?' she said simply.

She felt far from him. The undertone of his words repelled her and she withdrew her adoration for the Divers from the profanity of his bitterness. She was glad he was not next to her at dinner and she was still thinking of his words 'especially her' as they moved toward the table in the garden.

For a moment now she was beside Dick Diver on the path. Alongside his hard, neat brightness everything faded into the surety that he knew everything. For a year, which was for ever, she had had money and a certain celebrity and contact with the celebrated, and these latter had presented themselves merely as powerful enlargements of the people with whom the doctor's widow and her daughter had associated in a hôtel-pension in Paris. Rosemary was a romantic and her career had not provided many satisfactory opportunities on that score. Her mother, with the idea of a career for Rosemary, would not tolerate any such spurious substitutes as the excitations available on all sides, and indeed Rosemary was already beyond that – she was In the movies but not at all At them. So when she had seen approval of Dick Diver in her mother's face it meant that he was 'the real thing'; it meant permission to go as far as she could.

'I was watching you,' he said, and she knew he meant it. 'We've grown very fond of you.'

'I fell in love with you the first time I saw you,' she said quietly.

He pretended not to have heard, as if the compliment were purely formal.

'New friends,' he said, as if it were an important point, 'can often have a better time together than old friends.'

With that remark, which she did not understand precisely, she found herself at the table, picked out by slowly emerging lights against the dark dust. A chord of delight struck inside her when she saw that Dick had taken her mother on his right hand; for herself she was between Luis Campion and Brady.

Surcharged with her emotion she turned to Brady with the intention of confiding in him, but at her first mention of Dick a hard-boiled sparkle in his eyes gave her to understand that he refused the fatherly office. In turn she was equally firm when he tried to monopolize her hand, so they talked shop or rather she listened while he talked shop, her polite eyes never leaving his face, but her mind was so definitely elsewhere that she felt he must guess the fact. Intermittently she caught the gist of his sentences and supplied the rest from her subconscious, as one picks up the striking of a clock in the middle with only the rhythm of the first uncounted strokes lingering in the mind.

II

IN A PAUSE Rosemary looked away and up the table where Nicole sat between Tommy Barban and Abe North; her chow's hair foaming and frothing in the candlelight. Rosemary listened, caught sharply by the rich clipped voice in infrequent speech:

'The poor man,' Nicole exclaimed. 'Why did you want to saw him in two?'

'Naturally I wanted to see what was inside a waiter. Wouldn't you like to know what was inside a waiter?'

'Old menus,' suggested Nicole with a short laugh. 'Pieces of broken china and tips and pencil stubs.'

'Exactly – but the thing was to prove it scientifically. And of course doing it with that musical saw would have eliminated any sordidness.'

'Did you intend to play the saw while you performed the operation?' Tommy inquired.

'We didn't get quite that far. We were alarmed by the screams. We thought he might rupture something.'

'All sounds very peculiar to me,' said Nicole. 'Any musician that'll use another musician's saw to—'

They had been at table half an hour and a perceptible change had set in – person by person had given up something, a preoccupation, an anxiety, a suspicion, and now they were only their best selves and the Divers' guests. Not to have been friendly and interested would have seemed to reflect on the Divers, so now they were all trying, and seeing this, Rosemary liked everyone – except McKisco, who had contrived to be the unassimilated member of the party. This was less from ill will than from his determination to sustain with wine the good spirit he had enjoyed on his arrival. Lying back in his place between Earl Brady, to whom he had addressed several withering remarks about the movies, and Mrs Abrams, to whom he said nothing, he stared at Dick Diver with an expression of devastating irony, the effect being occasionally interrupted by his attempts to engage Dick in a cater-cornered conversation across the table.

'Aren't you a friend of Van Buren Denby?' he would say.

'I don't believe I know him.'

'I thought you were a friend of his,' he persisted irritably.

When the subject of Mr Denby fell of its own weight, he essayed other equally irrelative themes, but each time the very deference of Dick's attention seemed to paralyze him, and after a moment's stark pause the conversation that he had interrupted would go on without him. He tried breaking into other dialogues, but it was like continually shaking hands with a glove from which the hand had been withdrawn – so finally, with a resigned air of being among children, he devoted his attention entirely to the champagne. Rosemary's glance moved at intervals around the table, eager for the others' enjoyment, as if they were her future stepchildren. A gracious table light, emanating from a bowl of spicy pinks, fell upon Mrs Abrams' face, cooked to a turn in Veuve Cliquot, full of vigour, tolerance, adolescent good will; next to her sat Mr Royal

Dumphry, his girl's comeliness less startling in the pleasure world of evening. Then Violet McKisco, whose prettiness had been piped to the surface of her, so that she ceased her struggle to make tangible to herself her shadowy position as the wife of an arriviste who had not arrived.

Then came Dick, with his arms full of the slack he had taken up from others, deeply merged in his own party.

Then her mother, for ever perfect.

Then Barban talking to her mother with an urbane fluency that made Rosemary like him again. Then Nicole. Rosemary saw her suddenly in a new way and found her one of the most beautiful people she had ever known. Her face, the face of a saint, a viking Madonna, shone through the faint motes that snowed across the candlelight, drew down its flush from the wine-coloured lanterns in the pine. She was still as still.

Abe North was talking to her about his moral code: 'Of course I've got one,' he insisted, '– a man can't live without a moral code. Mine is that I'm against the burning of witches. Whenever they burn a witch I get all hot under the collar.' Rosemary knew from Brady that he was a musican who after a brilliant and precocious start had composed nothing for seven years.

Next was Campion, managing somehow to restrain

his most blatant effeminacy, and even to visit upon those near him a certain disinterested motherliness. Then Mary North with a face so merry that it was impossible not to smile back into the white mirrors of her teeth – the whole area around her parted lips was a lovely little circle of delight.

Finally Brady, whose heartiness became, moment by moment, a social thing instead of a crude assertion and reassertion of his own mental health, and his preservation of it by a detachment from the frailties of others.

Rosemary, as dewy with belief as a child from one of Mrs Burnett's vicious tracts, had a conviction of homecoming, of a return from the derisive and salacious improvizations of the frontier. There were fireflies riding on the dark air and a dog baying on some low and faraway ledge of the cliff. The table seemed to have risen a little toward the sky like a mechanical dancing platform, giving the people around it a sense of being alone with each other in the dark universe, nourished by its only good, warmed by its only lights. And, as if a curious hushed laugh from Mrs McKisco were a signal that such a detachment from the world had been attained, the two Divers began suddenly to warm and glow and expand, as if to make up to their guests, already so subtly assured of their importance, so flattered with politeness, for anything they might still miss from that country well left behind. Just for a moment they seemed to speak to every one at the table, singly and together, assuring them of their friendliness, their affection. And for a moment the faces turned up toward them were like the faces of poor children at a Christmas tree. Then abruptly the table broke up – the moment when the guests had been daringly lifted above conviviality into the rarer atmosphere of sentiment was over before it could be irreverently breathed, before they had half realized it was there.

But the diffused magic of the hot sweet South had withdrawn into them – the soft-pawed night and the ghostly wash of the Mediterranean far below – the magic left these things and melted into the two Divers and became part of them. Rosemary watched Nicole pressing upon her mother a yellow evening bag she had admired, saying, 'I think things ought to belong to the people that like them' – and then sweeping into it all the yellow articles she could find, a pencil, a lipstick, a little notebook, 'because they all go together.'

Nicole disappeared and presently Rosemary noticed that Dick was no longer there; the guests distributed themselves in the garden or drifted in toward the terrace.

'Do you want,' Violet McKisco asked Rosemary, 'to go to the bathroom?'

Not at that precise moment.

'I want,' insisted Mrs McKisco, 'to go to the bathroom.' As a frank outspoken woman she walked toward the house, dragging her secret after her, while Rosemary looked after with reprobation. Earl Brady proposed that they walk down to the sea wall but she felt that this was her time to have a share of Dick Diver when he reappeared, so she stalled, listening to McKisco quarrel with Barban.

'Why do you want to fight the Soviets?' McKisco said. 'The greatest experiment ever made by humanity? And the Riff? It seems to me it would be more heroic to fight on the just side.'

'How do you find out which it is?' asked Barban dryly.

'Why – usually everybody intelligent knows.'

'Are you a Communist?'

'I'm a Socialist,' said McKisco, 'I sympathize with Russia.'

'Well, I'm a soldier,' Barban answered pleasantly. 'My business is to kill people. I fought against the Riff because I am a European, and I have fought the Communists because they want to take my property from me.'

'Of all the narrow-minded excuses.' McKisco looked around to establish a derisive liaison with someone else, but without success. He had no idea what he was up against in Barban, neither of the simplicity of the other man's bag of ideas nor the complexity of his training. McKisco knew what ideas were, and as his mind grew he was able to recognize and sort an increasing number of them – but faced by a man whom he considered 'dumb', one in whom he found no ideas he could recognize as such, and yet to whom he could not feel personally superior, he jumped at the conclusion that Barban was the end product of an archaic world, and as such, worthless. McKisco's contacts with the princely classes in America had impressed upon him their uncertain and fumbling snobbery, their delight in ignorance and their deliberate rudeness, all lifted from the English with no regard paid to factors that make English philistinism and rudeness purposeful, and applied in a land where a little knowledge and civility buy more then they do anywhere else – an attitude which reached its apogee in the 'Harvard manner' of about 1900. He thought that this Barban was of that type, and being drunk rashly forgot that he was in awe of him – this led up to the trouble in which he presently found himself.

Feeling vaguely ashamed for McKisco, Rosemary waited, placid but inwardly on fire, for Dick Diver's return. From her chair at the deserted table with Barban, McKisco, and Abe she looked up along the path edged with shadowy myrtle and fern to the stone terrace, and falling in love with her mother's profile against a lighted door, was about to go there when Mrs McKisco came hurrying down from the house.

She exuded excitement. In the very silence with which she pulled out a chair and sat down, her eyes staring, her mouth working a little, they all recognized a person cropfull of news, and her husband's 'What's the matter, Vi?' came naturally, as all eyes turned toward her.

'My dear –' she said at large, and then addressed Rosemary, 'my dear – it's nothing. I really can't say a word.'

'You are among friends,' said Abe.

'Well, upstairs I came upon a scene, my dears—'

Shaking her head cryptically she broke off just in time, for Tommy arose and addressed her politely but sharply:

'It's inadvisable to comment on what goes on in this house.'

III

VIOLET BREATHED LOUD and hard once and with an effort brought another expression into her face.

Dick came finally and with a sure instinct he separated Barban and the McKiscos and became excessively ignorant and inquisitive about literature with McKisco – thus giving the latter the moment of superiority which he required. The others helped him carry lamps up – who would not be pleased at carrying lamps helpfully through the darkness? Rosemary helped, meanwhile responding patiently to Royal Dumphry's inexhaustible curiosity about Hollywood.

Now – she was thinking – I've earned a time alone with him. He must know that because his laws are like the laws Mother taught me.

Rosemary was right – presently he detached her from the company on the terrace, and they were alone together, borne away from the house toward the seaside wall with what were less steps than irregularly spaced intervals through some of which she was pulled, through others blown.

They looked out over the Mediterranean. Far below, the last excursion boat from the Iles des Lérins floated across the bay like a Fourth-of-July balloon foot-loose in the heavens. Between the black isles it floated, softly parting the dark tide.

'I understand why you speak as you do of your mother,' he said. 'Her attitude toward you is very fine, I think. She has a sort of wisdom that's rare in America.'

'Mother is perfect,' she prayed.

'I was talking to her about a plan I have – she told me that how long you both stayed in France depended on you.'

On *you*, Rosemary all but said aloud.

'So since things are over down here—'

'Over?' she inquired.

'Well, this is over – this part of the summer is over. Last week Nicole's sister left, tomorrow Tommy Barban leaves, Monday Abe and Mary North are leaving. Maybe we'll have more fun this summer but this particular fun is over. I want it to die violently instead of fading out sentimentally – that's why I gave this party. What I'm coming to is – Nicole and I are going up to Paris to see Abe North off for America – I wonder if you'd like to go with us.'

'What did Mother say?'

'She seemed to think it would be fine. She doesn't want to go herself. She wants you to go alone.'

'I haven't seen Paris since I've been grown,' said Rosemary. 'I'd love to see it with you.'

'That's nice of you.' Did she imagine that his voice was suddenly metallic? 'Of course we've been excited about you from the moment you came on the beach. That vitality, we were sure it was professional – especially Nicole was. It'd never use itself up on any one person or group.'

Her instinct cried out to her that he was passing her along slowly toward Nicole and she put her own brakes on, saying with an equal hardness:

'I wanted to know all of you too – especially you. I told you I fell in love with you the first time I saw you.'

She was right going at it that way. But the space between heaven and earth had cooled his mind, destroyed the impulsiveness that had led him to bring her here, and made him aware of the too obvious appeal, the struggle with an unrehearsed scene and unfamiliar words.

He tried now to make her want to go back to the house and it was difficult, and he did not quite want to lose her. She felt only the draught blowing as he joked with her good-humouredly.

'You don't know what you want. You go and ask your mother what you want.'

She was stricken. She touched him, feeling the smooth cloth of his dark coat like a chasuble. She seemed about to fall to her knees – from that position she delivered her last shot.

'I think you're the most wonderful person I ever met – except my mother.'

'You have romantic eyes.'

His laughter swept them on up toward the terrace where he delivered her to Nicole . . .

Too soon it had become time to go and the Divers helped them all to go quickly. In the Divers' big Isotta there would be Tommy Barban and his baggage – he was spending the night at the hotel to catch an early train – with Mrs Abrams, the McKiscos and Campion. Earl Brady was going to drop Rosemary and her mother on his way to Monte Carlo, and Royal

Dumphry rode with them because the Divers' car was crowded. Down in the garden lanterns still glowed over the table where they had dined, as the Divers stood side by side in the gate, Nicole blooming away and filling the night with graciousness, and Dick bidding good-bye to everyone by name. To Rosemary it seemed very poignant to drive away and leave them in their house. Again she wondered what Mrs McKisco had seen in the bathroom.

3

Bernice Bobs her Hair

I

AFTER DARK ON Saturday night one could stand on the first tee of the golf-course and see the country-club windows as a yellow expanse over a very black and wavy ocean. The waves of this ocean, so to speak, were the heads of many curious caddies, a few of the more ingenious chauffeurs, the golf professional's deaf sister – and there were usually several stray, diffident waves who might have rolled inside had they so desired. This was the gallery.

The balcony was inside. It consisted of the circle of wicker chairs that lined the wall of the combination clubroom and ballroom. At these Saturday-night dances it was largely feminine; a great babel of middle-aged ladies with sharp eyes and icy hearts behind lorgnettes and large bosoms. The main function of the balcony was critical, it occasionally showed grudging admiration, but never approval, for it is well known among ladies over thirty-five that when the younger set dance in the summer-time it is with the very worst intentions in the world, and if they are not bombarded with stony eyes stray couples will dance weird barbaric interludes in the corners, and the more popular, more dangerous, girls will sometimes be kissed in the parked limousines of unsuspecting dowagers.

But, after all, this critical circle is not close enough to the stage to see the actors' faces and catch the subtler byplay. It can only frown and lean, ask questions and make satisfactory deductions from its set of postulates, such as the one which states that every young man with a large income leads the life of a hunted partridge. It never really appreciates the drama of the shifting, semi-cruel world of adolescence. No; boxes, orchestra-circle, principals, and chorus be represented by the medley of faces and voices that sway to the plaintive African rhythm of Dyer's dance orchestra.

From sixteen-year-old Otis Ormonde, who has two more years at Hill School, to G. Reece Stoddard, over whose bureau at home hangs a Harvard law diploma; from little Madeleine Hogue, whose hair still feels strange and uncomfortable on top of her head, to Bessie MacRae, who has been the life of the party a little too long – more than ten years – the medley is not only the centre of the stage but contains the only people capable of getting an unobstructed view of it.

With a flourish and a bang the music stops. The couples exchange artificial, effortless smiles, facetiously repeat '*la*-de-*da*-*da* dum-*dum*,' and then the clatter of young feminine voices soars over the burst of clapping.

A few disappointed stags caught in midfloor as they had been about to cut in subsided listlessly back to the walls, because this was not like the riotous Christmas dances – these summer hops were considered just pleasantly warm and exciting, where even the younger marrieds rose and performed ancient waltzes and terrifying fox trots to the tolerant amusement of their younger brothers and sisters.

Warren McIntyre, who casually attended Yale, being one of the unfortunate stags, felt in his dinner-coat pocket for a cigarette and strolled out onto the wide, semidark veranda, where couples were scattered at tables, filling the lantern-hung night with vague words and hazy laughter. He nodded here and there at the less absorbed and as he passed each couple some half-forgotten fragment of a story played in his mind, for it was not a large city and everyone was Who's Who to everyone else's past. There, for example, were Jim Strain and Ethel Demorest, who had been privately engaged for three years. Every one knew that as soon as Jim managed to hold a job for more than two months she would marry him. Yet how bored they both looked, and how wearily Ethel regarded Jim sometimes, as if she wondered why she had trained the vines of her affection on such a wind-shaken poplar.

Warren was nineteen and rather pitying with those of his friends who hadn't gone East to college. But, like most boys, he bragged tremendously about the girls of his city when he was away from it. There was Genevieve Ormonde, who regularly made the rounds of dances, house-parties, and football games at Princeton, Yale, Williams, and Cornell; there was black-eyed Roberta Dillon, who was quite as famous to her own generation as Hiram Johnson or Ty Cobb; and, of course, there was Marjorie Harvey, who besides having a fairylike face and a dazzling, bewildering tongue was already justly celebrated for having turned five cart-wheels in succession during the last pump-and-slipper dance at New Haven.

Warren, who had grown up across the street from Marjorie, had long been 'crazy about her'. Sometimes she seemed to reciprocate his feeling with a faint gratitude, but she had tried him by her infallible test and informed him gravely that she did not love him. Her test was that when she was away from him she forgot him and had affairs with other boys. Warren found this discouraging, especially as Marjorie had been making little trips all summer, and for the first two or three days after each arrival home he saw great heaps of mail on the Harveys' hall table addressed to her in various masculine handwritings. To make matters worse, all during the month of August she had been visited by her cousin Bernice from Eau Claire, and it seemed impossible to see her alone. It was always necessary to hunt round and find someone to take care of Bernice. As August waned this was becoming more and more difficult.

Much as Warren worshipped Marjorie he had to admit that Cousin Bernice was sorta dopeless. She was pretty, with dark hair and high colour, but she was no fun on a party. Every Saturday night he danced a long arduous duty dance with her to please Marjorie, but he had never been anything but bored in her company.

'Warren' – a soft voice at his elbow broke in upon his thoughts, and he turned to see Marjorie, flushed and radiant as usual. She laid a hand on his shoulder and a glow settled almost imperceptibly over him.

'Warren,' she whispered 'do something for me – dance with Bernice. She's been stuck with little Otis Ormonde for almost an hour.'

Warren's glow faded.

'Why – sure,' he answered half-heartedly.

'You don't mind, do you? I'll see that you don't get stuck.'

''Sall right.'

Marjorie smiled – that smile that was thanks enough.

'You're an angel, and I'm obliged loads.'

With a sigh the angel glanced round the veranda, but Bernice and Otis were not in sight. He wandered back inside, and there in front of the women's dressing-room he found Otis in the centre of a group of young men who were convulsed with laughter. Otis was brandishing a piece of timber he had picked up, and discoursing volubly.

'She's gone in to fix her hair,' he announced wildly. 'I'm waiting to dance another hour with her.'

Their laughter was renewed.

'Why don't some of you cut in?' cried Otis resentfully. 'She likes more variety.'

'Why, Otis,' suggested a friend 'you've just barely got used to her.'

'Why the two-by-four, Otis?' inquired Warren, smiling.

'The two-by-four? Oh, this? This is a club. When she comes out I'll hit her on the head and knock her in again.'

Warren collapsed on a settee and howled with glee.

'Never mind, Otis,' he articulated finally. 'I'm relieving you this time.'

Otis simulated a sudden fainting attack and handed the stick to Warren.

'If you need it, old man,' he said hoarsely.

No matter how beautiful or brilliant a girl may be, the reputation of not being frequently cut in on makes her position at a dance unfortunate. Perhaps boys prefer her company to that of the butterflies with whom they dance a dozen times an evening, but youth in this jazz-nourished generation is temperamentally restless, and the idea of fox-trotting more than one full fox trot with the same girl is distasteful, not to say odious. When it comes to several dances and the intermissions between she can be quite sure that a young man, once relieved, will never tread on her wayward toes again.

Warren danced the next full dance with Bernice, and finally, thankful for the intermission, he led her to a table on the veranda. There was a moment's silence while she did unimpressive things with her fan.

'It's hotter here than in Eau Claire,' she said.

Warren stifled a sigh and nodded. It might be for all he knew or cared. He wondered idly whether she was a poor conversationalist because she got no attention or got no attention because she was a poor conversationalist.

'You going to be here much longer?' he asked and

then turned rather red. She might suspect his reasons for asking.

'Another week,' she answered, and stared at him as if to lunge at his next remark when it left his lips.

Warren fidgeted. Then with a sudden charitable impulse he decided to try part of his line on her. He turned and looked at her eyes.

'You've got an awfully kissable mouth,' he began quietly.

This was a remark that he sometimes made to girls at college proms when they were talking in just such half dark as this. Bernice distinctly jumped. She turned an ungraceful red and became clumsy with her fan. No one had ever made such a remark to her before.

'Fresh!' – the word had slipped out before she realized it, and she bit her lip. Too late she decided to be amused, and offered him a flustered smile.

Warren was annoyed. Though not accustomed to have that remark taken seriously, still it usually provoked a laugh or a paragraph of sentimental banter. And he hated to be called fresh, except in a joking way. His charitable impulse died and he switched the topic.

'Jim Strain and Ethel Demorest sitting out as usual,' he commented.

This was more in Bernice's line, but a faint regret mingled with her relief as the subject changed. Men did not talk to her about kissable mouths, but she knew that they talked in some such way to other girls.

'Oh, yes,' she said, and laughed. 'I hear they've been mooning around for years without a red penny. Isn't it silly?'

Warren's disgust increased. Jim Strain was a close friend of his brother's, and anyway he considered it bad form to sneer at people for not having money. But Bernice had had no intention of sneering. She was merely nervous.

II

When Marjorie and Bernice reached home at half after midnight they said good night at the top of the stairs. Though cousins, they were not intimates. As a matter of fact Marjorie had no female intimates – she considered girls stupid. Bernice on the contrary all through this parent-arranged visit had rather longed to exchange those confidences flavoured with giggles and tears that she considered an indispensable factor in all feminine intercourse. But in this respect she found Marjorie rather cold; felt somehow the same difficulty in talking to her that she had in talking to men. Marjorie never giggled, was never frightened, seldom embarrassed, and in fact had very few of the qualities which Bernice considered appropriately and blessedly feminine.

As Bernice busied herself with tooth-brush and

paste this night she wondered for the hundredth time why she never had any attention when she was away from home. That her family were the wealthiest in Eau Claire; that her mother entertained tremendously, gave little dinners for her daughter before all dances and bought her a car of her own to drive round in, never occurred to her as factors in her home-town social success. Like most girls she had been brought up on the warm milk prepared by Annie Fellows Johnston and on novels in which the female was beloved because of certain mysterious womanly qualities, always mentioned but never displayed.

Bernice felt a vague pain that she was not at present engaged in being popular. She did not know that had it not been for Marjorie's campaigning she would have danced the entire evening with one man; but she knew that even in Eau Claire other girls with less position and less pulchritude were given a much bigger rush. She attributed this to something subtly unscrupulous in those girls. It had never worried her, and if it had her mother would have assured her that the other girls cheapened themselves and that men really respected girls like Bernice.

She turned out the light in her bathroom, and on an impulse decided to go in and chat for a moment with her aunt Josephine, whose light was still on. Her soft slippers bore her noiselessly down the carpeted hall, but hearing voices inside she stopped near the partly opened door. Then she caught her own name, and without any definite intention of eavesdropping lingered – and the thread of the conversation going on inside pierced her consciousness sharply as if it had been drawn through with a needle.

'She's absolutely hopeless!' It was Marjorie's voice. 'Oh, I know what you're going to say! So many people have told you how pretty and sweet she is, and how she can cook! What of it? She has a bum time. Men don't like her.'

'What's a little cheap popularity?'

Mrs Harvey sounded annoyed.

'It's everything when you're eighteen,' said Marjorie emphatically. 'I've done my best. I've been polite and I've made men dance with her, but they just won't stand being bored. When I think of that gorgeous colouring wasted on such a ninny, and think what Martha Carey could do with it – oh!'

'There's no courtesy these days.'

Mrs Harvey's voice implied that modern situations were too much for her. When she was a girl all young ladies who belonged to nice families had glorious times.

'Well,' said Marjorie, 'no girl can permanently bolster up a lame-duck visitor, because these days it's every girl for herself. I've even tried to drop hints about clothes and things, and she's been furious – given me the funniest looks. She's sensitive enough to know she's not getting away with much, but I'll bet she consoles herself by thinking that she's very virtuous and that I'm too gay and fickle and will come to a bad end. All unpopular girls think that way. Sour grapes! Sarah Hopkins refers to Genevieve and Roberta and me as gardenia girls! I'll bet she'd give ten years of her life and her European education to be a gardenia girl and have three or four men in love with her and be cut in on every few feet at dances.'

'It seems to me,' interrupted Mrs Harvey rather wearily, 'that you ought to be able to do something for Bernice. I know she's not very vivacious.'

Marjorie groaned.

'Vivacious! Good grief! I've never heard her say anything to a boy except that it's hot or the floor's crowded or that she's going to school in New York next year. Sometimes she asks them what kind of car they have and tells them the kind she has. Thrilling!'

There was a short silence and then Mrs Harvey took up her refrain:

'All I know is that other girls not half so sweet and attractive get partners. Martha Carey, for instance, is stout and loud, and her mother is distinctly common. Roberta Dillon is so thin this year that she looks as though Arizona were the place for her. She's dancing herself to death.'

'But, mother,' objected Marjorie impatiently,

'Martha is cheerful and awfully witty and an awfully slick girl, and Roberta's a marvellous dancer. She's been popular for ages!'

Mrs Harvey yawned.

'I think it's that crazy Indian blood in Bernice,' continued Marjorie. 'Maybe she's a reversion to type. Indian women all just sat round and never said anything.'

'Go to bed, you silly child,' laughed Mrs Harvey. 'I wouldn't have told you that if I'd thought you were going to remember it. And I think most of your ideas are perfectly idiotic,' she finished sleepily.

There was another silence, while Marjorie considered whether or not convincing her mother was worth the trouble. People over forty can seldom be permanently convinced of anything. At eighteen our convictions are hills from which we look; at forty-five they are caves in which we hide.

Having decided this, Marjorie said good night. When she came out into the hall it was quite empty.

III

WHILE MARJORIE WAS breakfasting late next day Bernice came into the room with a rather formal good morning, sat down opposite, stared intently over and slightly moistened her lips.

'What's on your mind?' inquired Marjorie, rather puzzled.

Bernice paused before she threw her hand-grenade.

'I heard what you said about me to your mother last night.'

Marjorie was startled, but she showed only a faintly heightened colour and her voice was quite even when she spoke.

'Where were you?'

'In the hall. I didn't mean to listen – at first.'

After an involuntary look of contempt Marjorie dropped her eyes and became very interested in balancing a stray corn-flake on her finger.

'I guess I'd better go back to Eau Claire – if I'm such a nuisance.' Bernice's lower lip was trembling violently and she continued on a wavering note: 'I've tried to be nice, and – and I've been first neglected and then insulted. No one ever visited me and got such treatment.'

Marjorie was silent.

'But I'm in the way, I see. I'm a drag on you. Your friends don't like me.' She paused, and then remembered another one of her grievances. 'Of course I was furious last week when you tried to hint to me that that dress was unbecoming. Don't you think I know how to dress myself?'

'No,' murmured Marjorie less than half-aloud.

'What?'

'I didn't hint anything,' said Marjorie succinctly. 'I said, as I remember, that it was better to wear a becoming dress three times straight than to alternate it with two frights.'

'Do you think that was a very nice thing to say?'

'I wasn't trying to be nice.' Then after a pause: 'When do you want to go?'

Bernice drew in her breath sharply.

'Oh!' It was a little half-cry.

Marjorie looked up in surprise.

'Didn't you say you were going?'

'Yes, but—'

'Oh, you were only bluffing!'

They stared at each other across the breakfast-table for a moment. Misty waves were passing before Bernice's eyes, while Marjorie's face wore that rather hard expression that she used when slightly intoxicated undergraduate's were making love to her.

'So you were bluffing,' she repeated as if it were what she might have expected.

Bernice admitted it by bursting into tears. Marjorie's eyes showed boredom.

'You're my cousin,' sobbed Bernice. 'I'm v-v-visiting you. I was to stay a month, and if I go home my mother will know and she'll wah-wonder—'

Marjorie waited until the shower of broken words collapsed into little sniffles.

'I'll give you my month's allowance,' she said

coldly, 'and you can spend this last week anywhere you want. There's a very nice hotel—'

Bernice's sobs rose to a flute note, and rising of a sudden she fled from the room.

An hour later, while Marjorie was in the library absorbed in composing one of those non-committal marvellously elusive letters that only a young girl can write, Bernice reappeared, very red-eyed, and consciously calm. She cast no glance at Marjorie but took a book at random from the shelf and sat down as if to read. Marjorie seemed absorbed in her letter and continued writing. When the clock showed noon Bernice closed her book with a snap.

'I suppose I'd better get my railroad ticket.'

This was not the beginning of the speech she had rehearsed upstairs, but as Marjorie was not getting her cues – wasn't urging her to be reasonable; it's all a mistake – it was the best opening she could muster.

'Just wait till I finish this letter,' said Marjorie without looking round. 'I want to get it off in the next mail.'

After another minute, during which her pen scratched busily, she turned round and relaxed with an air of 'at your service'. Again Bernice had to speak.

'Do you want me to go home?'

'Well,' said Marjorie, considering, 'I suppose if you're not having a good time you'd better go. No use being miserable.'

'Don't you think common kindness—'

'Oh, please don't quote "Little Women"!' cried Marjorie impatiently. 'That's out of style.'

'You think so?'

'Heavens, yes! What modern girl could live like those inane females?'

'They were the models for our mothers.'

Marjorie laughed.

'Yes, they were – not! Besides, our mothers were all very well in their way, but they know very little about their daughters' problems.'

Bernice drew herself up.

'Please don't talk about my mother.'

Marjorie laughed.

'I don't think I mentioned her.'

Bernice felt that she was being led away from her subject.

'Do you think you've treated me very well?'

'I've done my best. You're rather hard material to work with.'

The lids of Bernice's eyes reddened.

'I think you're hard and selfish, and you haven't a feminine quality in you.'

'Oh, my Lord!' cried Marjorie in desperation 'You little nut! Girls like you are responsible for all the tiresome colourless marriages; all those ghastly inefficiencies that pass as feminine qualities. What a blow it must be when a man with imagination marries the beautiful bundle of clothes that he's been building ideals round, and finds that she's just a weak, whining, cowardly mass of affectations!'

Bernice's mouth had slipped half open.

'The womanly woman!' continued Marjorie. 'Her whole early life is occupied in whining criticisms of girls like me who really do have a good time.'

Bernice's jaw descended farther as Marjorie's voice rose.

'There's some excuse for an ugly girl whining. If I'd been irretrievably ugly I'd never have forgiven my parents for bringing me into the world. But you're starting life without any handicap –' Marjorie's little fist clinched. 'If you expect me to weep with you you'll be disappointed. Go or stay, just as you like.' And picking up her letters she left the room.

Bernice claimed a headache and failed to appear at luncheon. They had a matinée date for the afternoon, but the headache persisting, Marjorie made explanations to a not very downcast boy. But when she returned late in the afternoon she found Bernice with a strangely set face waiting for her in her bedroom.

'I've decided,' began Bernice without preliminaries, 'that maybe you're right about things – possibly not. But if you'll tell me why your friends aren't – aren't interested in me I'll see if I can do what you want me to.'

Marjorie was at the mirror shaking down her hair.

'Do you mean it?'

'Yes.'

'Without reservations? Will you do exactly what I say?'

'Well, I—'

'Well nothing! Will you do exactly as I say?'

'If they're sensible things.'

'They're not! You're no case for sensible things.'

'Are you going to make – to recommend—'

'Yes, everything. If I tell you to take boxing lessons you'll have to do it. Write home and tell your mother you're going to stay another two weeks.'

'If you'll tell me—'

'All right – I'll just give you a few examples now. First you have no ease of manner. Why? Because you're never sure about your personal appearance. When a girl feels that she's perfectly groomed and dressed she can forget that part of her. That's charm. The more parts of yourself you can afford to forget the more charm you have.'

'Don't I look all right?'

'No; for instance you never take care of your eyebrows. They're black and lustrous, but by leaving them straggly they're a blemish. They'd be beautiful if you'd take care of them in one-tenth the time you take doing nothing. You're going to brush them so that they'll grow straight.'

Bernice raised the brows in question.

'Do you mean to say that men notice eyebrows?'

'Yes – subconsciously. And when you go home you ought to have your teeth straightened a little. It's almost imperceptible, still—'

'But I thought,' interrupted Bernice in bewilderment, 'that you despised little dainty feminine things like that.'

'I hate dainty minds,' answered Marjorie. 'But a girl has to be dainty in person. If she looks like a million dollars she can talk about Russia, ping-pong, or the League of Nations and get away with it.'

'What else?'

'Oh, I'm just beginning! There's your dancing.'

'Don't I dance all right?'

'No, you don't – you lean on a man; yes, you do – ever so slightly. I noticed it when we were dancing together yesterday. And you dance standing up straight instead of bending over a little. Probably some old lady on the side-line once told you that you looked so dignified that way. But except with a very small girl it's much harder on the man, and he's the one that counts.'

'Go on.' Bernice's brain was reeling.

'Well, you've got to learn to be nice to men who are sad birds. You look as if you'd been insulted whenever you're thrown with any except the most popular boys. Why, Bernice, I'm cut in on every few feet – and who does most of it? Why, those very sad birds. No girl can afford to neglect them. They're the big part of any crowd. Young boys too shy to talk are the very best conversational practice. Clumsy boys are the best dancing practice. If you can follow them and yet look graceful you can follow a baby tank across a barb-wire sky-scraper.'

Bernice sighed profoundly, but Marjorie was not through.

'If you go to a dance and really amuse, say, three sad birds that dance with you; if you talk so well to them that they forget they're stuck with you, you've done something. They'll come back next time, and gradually so many sad birds will dance with you that the attractive boys will see there's no danger of being stuck – then they'll dance with you.'

'Yes,' agreed Bernice faintly. 'I think I begin to see.'

'And finally,' concluded Marjorie, 'poise and charm will just come. You'll wake up some morning knowing you've attained it and men will know it too.'

Bernice rose.

'It's been awfully kind of you – but nobody's ever talked to me like this before, and I feel sort of startled.'

Marjorie made no answer but gazed pensively at her own image in the mirror.

'You're a peach to help me,' continued Bernice.

Still Marjorie did not answer, and Bernice thought she had seemed too grateful.

'I know you don't like sentiment,' she said timidly.

Marjorie turned to her quickly.

'Oh, I wasn't thinking about that. I was considering whether we hadn't better bob your hair.'

Bernice collapsed backward upon the bed.

IV

ON THE FOLLOWING Wednesday evening there was a dinner-dance at the country club. When the guests strolled in Bernice found her place-card with a slight feeling of irritation. Though at her right sat G. Reece Stoddard, a most desirable and distinguished young bachelor, the all-important left held only Charley Paulson. Charley lacked height, beauty, and social shrewdness, and in her new enlightenment Bernice decided that his only qualification to be her partner was that he had never been stuck with her. But this feeling of irritation left with the last of the soup-plates, and Marjorie's specific instruction came to her. Swallowing her pride she turned to Charley Paulson and plunged.

'Do you think I ought to bob my hair, Mr Charley Paulson?'

Charley looked up in surprise.

'Why?'

'Because I'm considering it. It's such a sure and easy way of attracting attention.'

Charley smiled pleasantly. He could not know this had been rehearsed. He replied that he didn't know much about bobbed hair. But Bernice was there to tell him.

'I want to be a society vampire, you see,' she announced coolly, and went on to inform him that bobbed hair was the necessary prelude. She added that she wanted to ask his advice, because she had heard he was so critical about girls.

Charley, who knew as much about the psychology of women as he did of the mental states of Buddhist contemplatives, felt vaguely flattered.

'So I've decided,' she continued, her voice rising slightly, 'that early next week I'm going down to the Sevier Hotel barber-shop, sit in the first chair, and get my hair bobbed.' She faltered noticing that the people near her had paused in their conversation and were listening; but after a confused second Marjorie's coaching told, and she finished her paragraph to the vicinity at large. 'Of course I'm charging admission, but if you'll all come down and encourage me I'll issue passes for the inside seats.'

There was a ripple of appreciative laughter, and under cover of it G. Reece Stoddard leaned over quickly and said close to her ear: 'I'll take a box right now.'

She met his eyes and smiled as if he had said something surprisingly brilliant.

'Do you believe in bobbed hair?' asked G. Reece in the same undertone.

'I think it's unmoral,' affirmed Bernice gravely. 'But, of course, you've either got to amuse people or feed 'em or shock 'em.' Marjorie had culled this from Oscar Wilde. It was greeted with a ripple of laughter from the men and a series of quick, intent looks from the girls. And then as though she had said nothing of wit or moment Bernice turned again to Charley and spoke confidentially in his ear.

'I want to ask you your opinion of several people. I imagine you're a wonderful judge of character.'

Charley thrilled faintly – paid her a subtle compliment by overturning her water.

Two hours later, while Warren McIntyre was standing passively in the stag line abstractedly watching the dancers and wondering whither and with whom Marjorie had disappeared, an unrelated perception began to creep slowly upon him – a perception that Bernice, cousin to Marjorie, had been cut in on several times in the past five minutes. He closed his eyes, opened them and looked again. Several minutes back she had been dancing with a visiting boy, a matter easily accounted for; a visiting boy would know no better. But now she was dancing with someone else, and there was Charley Paulson headed for her with enthusiastic determination in his eye. Funny – Charley seldom danced with more than three girls an evening.

Warren was distinctly surprised when – the exchange having been effected – the man relieved proved to be none other than G. Reece Stoddard himself. And G. Reece seemed not at all jubilant at being relieved. Next time Bernice danced near, Warren regarded her intently. Yes, she was pretty, distinctly pretty; and tonight her face seemed really vivacious. She had that look that no woman, however histrionically proficient, can successfully counterfeit – she looked as if she were having a good time. He liked the way she had her hair arranged, wondered if it was brilliantine that made it glisten so. And that dress was becoming – a dark red that set off her shadowy eyes and high colouring. He remembered that he had thought her pretty when she first came to town, before he had realized that she was dull. Too bad she was dull – dull girls unbearable – certainly pretty though.

His thoughts zigzagged back to Marjorie. This disappearance would be like other disappearances. When she reappeared he would demand where she had been – would be told emphatically that it was none of his business. What a pity she was so sure of him! She basked in the knowledge that no other girl in town interested him; she defied him to fall in love with Genevieve or Roberta.

Warren sighed. The way to Marjorie's affections was a labyrinth indeed. He looked up. Bernice was again dancing with the visiting boy. Half unconsciously he took a step out from the stag line in her direction, and hesitated. Then he said to himself that it was charity. He walked towards her – collided suddenly with G. Reece Stoddard.

'Pardon me,' said Warren.

But G. Reece had not stopped to apologize. He had again cut in on Bernice.

That night at one o'clock Marjorie, with one hand on the electric-light switch in the hall, turned to take a last look at Bernice's sparkling eyes.

'So it worked?'

'Oh, Marjorie, yes!' cried Bernice.

'I saw you were having a gay time.'

'I did! The only trouble was that about midnight I ran short of talk. I had to repeat myself – with different men of course. I hope they won't compare notes.'

'Men don't,' said Marjorie, yawning, 'and it wouldn't matter if they did – they'd think you were even trickier.'

She snapped out the light, and as they started up the stairs Bernice grasped the banister thankfully.

For the first time in her life she had been danced tired.

'You see,' said Marjorie it the top of the stairs, 'one man sees another man cut in and he thinks there must be something there. Well, we'll fix up some new stuff tomorrow. Good night.'

'Good night.'

As Bernice took down her hair she passed the evening before her in review. She had followed instructions exactly. Even when Charley Paulson cut in for the eighth time she had simulated delight and had apparently been both interested and flattered. She had not talked about the weather or Eau Claire or automobiles or her school, but had confined her conversation to me, you, and us.

But a few minutes before she fell asleep a rebellious thought was churning drowsily in her brain – after all, it was she who had done it. Marjorie, to be sure, had given her her conversation, but then Marjorie got much of her conversation out of things she read. Bernice had bought the red dress, though she had never valued it highly before Marjorie dug it out of her trunk – and her own voice had said the words, her own lips had smiled, her own feet had danced. Marjorie nice girl – vain, though – nice evening – nice boys – like Warren – Warren – Warren – what's his name – Warren—

She fell asleep.

V

To Bernice the next week was a revelation. With the feeling that people really enjoyed looking at her and listening to her came the foundation of self-confidence. Of course there were numerous mistakes at first. She did not know, for instance, that Draycott Deyo was studying for the ministry; she was unaware that he had cut in on her because he thought she was a quiet, reserved girl. Had she known these things she would not have treated him to the line which began 'Hello, Shell Shock!' and continued with the bathtub story – 'It takes a frightful lot of energy to fix my hair in the summer – there's so much of it – so I always fix it first and powder my face and put on my hat; then I get into the bathtub, and dress afterward. Don't you think that's the best plan?'

Though Draycott Deyo was in the throes of difficulties concerning baptism by immersion and might possibly have seen a connection, it must be admitted that he did not. He considered feminine bathing an immoral subject, and gave her some of his ideas on the depravity of modern society.

But to offset that unfortunate occurrence Bernice had several signal successes to her credit. Little Otis Ormonde pleaded off from a trip East and elected instead to follow her with a puppylike devotion, to the amusement of his crowd and to the irritation of

G. Reece Stoddard, several of whose afternoon calls Otis completely ruined by the disgusting tenderness of the glances he bent on Bernice. He even told her the story of the two-by-four and the dressing-room to show her how frightfully mistaken he and every one else had been in their first judgment of her. Bernice laughed off that incident with a slight sinking sensation.

Of all Bernice's conversation perhaps the best known and most universally approved was the line about the bobbing of her hair.

'Oh, Bernice, when you goin' to get the hair bobbed?'

'Day after tomorrow maybe,' she would reply, laughing. 'Will you come and see me? Because I'm counting on you, you know.'

'Will we? You know! But you better hurry up.'

Bernice, whose tonsorial intentions were strictly dishonorable, would laugh again.

'Pretty soon now. You'd be surprised.'

But perhaps the most significant symbol of her success was the grey car of the hypercritical Warren McIntyre, parked daily in front of the Harvey house. At first the parlourmaid was distinctly startled when he asked for Bernice instead of Marjorie; after a week of it she told the cook that Miss Bernice had gotta holda Miss Marjorie's best fella.

And Miss Bernice had. Perhaps it began with

Warren's desire to rouse jealousy in Marjorie; perhaps it was the familiar though unrecognized strain of Marjorie in Bernice's conversation; perhaps it was both of these and something of sincere attraction besides. But somehow the collective mind of the younger set knew within a week that Marjorie's most reliable beau had made an amazing face-about and was giving an indisputable rush to Marjorie's guest. The question of the moment was how Marjorie would take it. Warren called Bernice on the phone twice a day, sent her notes, and they were frequently seen together in his roadster, obviously engrossed in one of those tense, significant conversations as to whether or not he was sincere.

Marjorie on being twitted only laughed. She said she was mighty glad that Warren had at last found someone who appreciated him. So the younger set laughed, too, and guessed that Marjorie didn't care and let it go at that.

One afternoon when there were only three days left of her visit Bernice was waiting in the hall for Warren, with whom she was going to a bridge party. She was in rather a blissful mood, and when Marjorie – also bound for the party – appeared beside her and began casually to adjust her hat in the mirror, Bernice was utterly unprepared for anything in the nature of a clash. Marjorie did her work very coldly and succinctly in three sentences.

'You may as well get Warren out of your head,' she said coldly.

'What?' Bernice was utterly astounded.

'You may as well stop making a fool of yourself over Warren McIntyre. He doesn't care a snap of his fingers about you.'

For a tense moment they regarded each other – Marjorie scornful, aloof; Bernice astounded, half-angry, half-afraid. Then two cars drove up in front of the house and there was a riotous honking. Both of them gasped faintly, turned, and side by side hurried out.

All through the bridge party Bernice strove in vain to master a rising uneasiness. She had offended Marjorie, the sphinx of sphinxes. With the most wholesome and innocent intentions in the world she had stolen Marjorie's property. She felt suddenly and horribly guilty. After the bridge game, when they sat in an informal circle and the conversation became general, the storm gradually broke. Little Otis Ormonde inadvertently precipitated it.

'When you going back to kindergarten, Otis?' someone had asked.

'Me? Day Bernice gets her hair bobbed.'

'Then your education's over,' said Marjorie quickly. 'That's only a bluff of hers. I should think you'd have realized.'

'That a fact?' demanded Otis, giving Bernice a reproachful glance.

Bernice's ears burned as she tried to think up an effectual comeback. In the face of this direct attack her imagination was paralysed.

'There's a lot of bluffs in the world,' continued Marjorie quite pleasantly. 'I should think you'd be young enough to know that, Otis.'

'Well,' said Otis, 'maybe so. But gee! With a line like Bernice's—'

'Really?' yawned Marjorie. 'What's her latest bon mot?'

No one seemed to know. In fact, Bernice, having trifled with her muse's beau, had said nothing memorable of late.

'Was that really all a line?' asked Roberta curiously.

Bernice hesitated. She felt that wit in some form was demanded of her, but under her cousin's suddenly frigid eyes she was completely incapacitated.

'I don't know,' she stalled.

'Splush!' said Marjorie. 'Admit it!'

Bernice saw that Warren's eyes had left a ukulele he had been tinkering with and were fixed on her questioningly.

'Oh, I don't know!' she repeated steadily. Her cheeks were glowing.

'Splush!' remarked Marjorie again.

'Come through, Bernice,' urged Otis. 'Tell her where to get off.'

Bernice looked round again – she seemed unable to get away from Warren's eyes.

'I like bobbed hair,' she said hurriedly, as if he had asked her a question, 'and I intend to bob mine.'

'When?' demanded Marjorie.

'Any time.'

'No time like the present,' suggested Roberta.

Otis jumped to his feet.

'Good stuff!' he cried. 'We'll have a summer bobbing party. Sevier Hotel barber-shop, I think you said.'

In an instant all were on their feet. Bernice's heart throbbed violently.

'What?' she gasped.

Out of the group came Marjorie's voice, very clear and contemptuous.

'Don't worry – she'll back out!'

'Come on, Bernice!' cried Otis, starting towards the door.

Four eyes – Warren's and Marjorie's – stared at her, challenged her, defied her. For another second she wavered wildly.

'All right,' she said swiftly. 'I don't care if I do.'

An eternity of minutes later, riding down-town through the late afternoon beside Warren, the others following in Roberta's car close behind, Bernice had all the sensations of Marie Antoinette bound for the guillotine in a tumbrel. Vaguely she wondered why she did not cry out that it was all a mistake. It was all she could do to keep from clutching her hair with both bands to protect it from the suddenly hostile world. Yet she did neither. Even the thought of her mother was no deterrent now. This was the test supreme of her sportsmanship; her right to walk unchallenged in the starry heaven of popular girls.

Warren was moodily silent, and when they came to the hotel he drew up at the curb and nodded to Bernice to precede him out. Roberta's car emptied a laughing crowd into the shop, which presented two bold plate-glass windows to the street.

Bernice stood on the curb and looked at the sign, Sevier Barber-Shop. It was a guillotine indeed, and the hangman was the first barber, who, attired in a white coat and smoking a cigarette, leaned nonchalantly against the first chair. He must have heard of her; he must have been waiting all week, smoking eternal cigarettes beside that portentous, too-often-mentioned first chair. Would they blindfold her? No, but they would tie a white cloth round her neck lest any of her blood – nonsense – hair – should get on her clothes.

'All right, Bernice,' said Warren quickly.

With her chin in the air she crossed the sidewalk, pushed open the swinging screen-door, and giving not a glance to the uproarious, riotous row that occupied the waiting bench, went up to the fat barber.

'I want you to bob my hair.'

The first barber's mouth slid somewhat open. His cigarette dropped to the floor.

'Huh?'

'My hair – bob it!'

Refusing further preliminaries, Bernice took her seat on high. A man in the chair next to her turned on his side and gave her a glance, half lather, half amazement. One barber started and spoiled little Willy Schuneman's monthly haircut. Mr O'Reilly in the last chair grunted and swore musically in ancient Gaelic as a razor bit into his cheek. Two bootblacks became wide-eyed and rushed for her feet. No, Bernice didn't care for a shine.

Outside a passer-by stopped and stared; a couple joined him; half a dozen small boys' noses sprang into life, flattened against the glass; and snatches of conversation borne on the summer breeze drifted in through the screen-door.

'Lookada long hair on a kid!'

'Where'd yuh get 'at stuff? 'At's a bearded lady he just finished shavin'.'

But Bernice saw nothing, heard nothing. Her only living sense told her that this man in the white coat had removed one tortoiseshell comb and then another; that his fingers were fumbling clumsily with unfamiliar hairpins; that this hair, this wonderful hair of hers, was going – she would never again feel its long voluptuous pull as it hung in a dark-brown glory down her back. For a second she was near breaking down, and then the picture before her swam mechanically into her vision – Marjorie's mouth curling in a faint ironic smile as if to say:

'Give up and get down! You tried to buck me and I called your bluff. You see you haven't got a prayer.'

And some last energy rose up in Bernice, for she clinched her hands under the white cloth, and there was a curious narrowing of her eyes that Marjorie remarked on to someone long afterward.

Twenty minutes later the barber swung her round to face the mirror, and she flinched at the full extent of the damage that had been wrought. Her hair was not curly and now it lay in lank lifeless blocks on both sides of her suddenly pale face. It was ugly as sin – she had known it would be ugly as sin. Her face's chief charm had been a Madonna-like simplicity. Now that was gone and she was – well frightfully mediocre – not stagy; only ridiculous, like a Greenwich Villager who had left her spectacles at home.

As she climbed down from the chair she tried to smile – failed miserably. She saw two of the girls exchange glances; noticed Marjorie's mouth curved in attenuated mockery – and that Warren's eyes were suddenly very cold.

'You see' – her words fell into an awkward pause – 'I've done it.'

'Yes, you've – done it,' admitted Warren.

'Do you like it?'

There was a half-hearted 'Sure' from two or three voices, another awkward pause, and then Marjorie turned swiftly and with serpentlike intensity to Warren.

'Would you mind running me down to the cleaners?' she asked. 'I've simply got to get a dress there before supper. Roberta's driving right home and she can take the others.'

Warren stared abstractedly at some infinite speck out the window. Then for an instant his eyes rested coldly on Bernice before they turned to Marjorie.

'Be glad to,' he said slowly.

VI

BERNICE DID NOT fully realize the outrageous trap that had been set for her until she met her aunt's amazed glance just before dinner.

'Why Bernice!'

'I've bobbed it, Aunt Josephine.'

'Why, child!'

'Do you like it?'

'Why Ber-nice!'

'I suppose I've shocked you.'

'No, but what'll Mrs Deyo think tomorrow night? Bernice, you should have waited until after the Deyo's dance – you should have waited if you wanted to do that.'

'It was sudden, Aunt Josephine. Anyway, why does it matter to Mrs Deyo particularly?'

'Why child,' cried Mrs Harvey, 'in her paper on "The Foibles of the Younger Generation" that she read at the last meeting of the Thursday Club she devoted fifteen minutes to bobbed hair. It's her pet abomination. And the dance is for you and Marjorie!'

'I'm sorry.'

'Oh, Bernice, what'll your mother say? She'll think I let you do it.'

'I'm sorry.'

Dinner was an agony. She had made a hasty attempt with a curling-iron, and burned her finger and much hair. She could see that her aunt was both worried and grieved, and her uncle kept saying, 'Well, I'll be darned!' over and over in a hurt and faintly hostile tone. And Marjorie sat very quietly, entrenched behind a faint smile, a faintly mocking smile.

Somehow she got through the evening. Three boy's called; Marjorie disappeared with one of them, and Bernice made a listless unsuccessful attempt to entertain the two others – sighed thankfully as she climbed the stairs to her room at half past ten. What a day!

When she had undressed for the night the door opened and Marjorie came in.

'Bernice,' she said 'I'm awfully sorry about the Deyo dance. I'll give you my word of honour I'd forgotten all about it.'

''Sall right,' said Bernice shortly. Standing before the mirror she passed her comb slowly through her short hair.

'I'll take you down-town tomorrow,' continued Marjorie, 'and the hairdresser'll fix it so you'll look slick. I didn't imagine you'd go through with it. I'm really mighty sorry.'

'Oh, 'sall right!'

'Still it's your last night, so I suppose it won't matter much.'

Then Bernice winced as Marjorie tossed her own hair over her shoulders and began to twist it slowly into two long blonde braids until in her cream-coloured négligé she looked like a delicate painting of some Saxon princess. Fascinated, Bernice watched the braids grow. Heavy and luxurious they were, moving under the supple fingers like restive snakes – and to Bernice remained this relic and the curling-iron and a tomorrow full of eyes. She could see G. Reece Stoddard, who liked her, assuming his Harvard manner and telling his dinner partner that Bernice shouldn't have been allowed to go to the movies so much; she could see Draycott Deyo exchanging glances with his mother and then being conscientiously charitable to her. But then perhaps by tomorrow

Mrs Deyo would have heard the news; would send round an icy little note requesting that she fail to appear – and behind her back they would all laugh and know that Marjorie had made a fool of her; that her chance at beauty had been sacrificed to the jealous whim of a selfish girl. She sat down suddenly before the mirror, biting the inside of her cheek.

'I like it,' she said with an effort. 'I think it'll be becoming.'

Marjorie smiled.

'It looks all right. For heaven's sake, don't let it worry you!'

'I won't.'

'Good night Bernice.'

But as the door closed something snapped within Bernice. She sprang dynamically to her feet, clenching her hands, then swiftly and noiselessly crossed over to her bed and from underneath it dragged out her suitcase. Into it she tossed toilet articles and a change of clothing, Then she turned to her trunk and quickly dumped in two drawerfuls of lingerie and summer dresses. She moved quietly, but with deadly efficiency, and in three-quarters of an hour her trunk was locked and strapped and she was fully dressed in a becoming new travelling suit that Marjorie had helped her pick out.

Sitting down at her desk she wrote a short note to Mrs Harvey, in which she briefly outlined her reasons for going. She sealed it, addressed it, and laid it on her pillow. She glanced at her watch. The train left at one, and she knew that if she walked down to the Marborough Hotel two blocks away she could easily get a taxicab.

Suddenly she drew in her breath sharply and an expression flashed into her eyes that a practised character reader might have connected vaguely with the set look she had worn in the barber's chair – somehow a development of it. It was quite a new look for Bernice – and it carried consequences.

She went stealthily to the bureau, picked up an article that lay there, and turning out all the lights stood quietly until her eyes became accustomed to the darkness. Softly she pushed open the door to Marjorie's room. She heard the quiet, even breathing of an untroubled conscience asleep.

She was by the bedside now, very deliberate and calm. She acted swiftly. Bending over she found one of the braids of Marjorie's hair, followed it up with her hand to the point nearest the head, and then holding it a little slack so that the sleeper would feel no pull, she reached down with the shears and severed it. With the pigtail in her hand she held her breath. Marjorie had muttered something in her sleep. Bernice deftly amputated the other braid, paused for an instant, and then flitted swiftly and silently back to her own room.

Downstairs she opened the big front door, closed it carefully behind her, and feeling oddly happy and exuberant stepped off the porch into the moonlight, swinging her heavy grip like a shopping-bag. After a minute's brisk walk she discovered that her left hand still held the two blond braids. She laughed unexpectedly – had to shut her mouth hard to keep from emitting an absolute peal. She was passing Warren's house now, and on the impulse she set down her baggage, and swinging the braids like pieces of rope flung them at the wooden porch, where they landed with a slight thud. She laughed again, no longer restraining herself.

'Huh,' she giggled wildly. 'Scalp the selfish thing!'

Then picking up her staircase she set off at a half-run down the moonlit street.

4

The Bridal Party

I

THERE WAS THE usual insincere little note saying: 'I wanted you to be the first to know.' It was a double shock to Michael, announcing, as it did, both the engagement and the imminent marriage; which, moreover, was to be held, not in New York, decently and far away, but here in Paris under his very nose, if that could be said to extend over the Protestant Episcopal Church of the Holy Trinity, Avenue George-Cinq. The date was two weeks off, early in June.

At first Michael was afraid and his stomach felt hollow. When he left the hotel that morning, the *femme de chambre*, who was in love with his fine, sharp profile and his pleasant buoyancy, scented the hard abstraction that had settled over him. He walked in a daze to his bank, he bought a detective story at Smith's on the Rue de Rivoli, he sympathetically stared for a while at a faded panorama of the battlefields in a tourist-office window and cursed a Greek tout who followed him with a half-displayed packet of innocuous post cards warranted to be very dirty indeed.

But the fear stayed with him, and after a while he recognized it as the fear that now he would never be happy. He had met Caroline Dandy when she was seventeen, possessed her young heart all through her first season in New York, and then lost her, slowly, tragically, uselessly, because he had no money and could make no money; because, with all the energy and good will in the world, he could not find himself; because, loving him still, Caroline had lost faith and begun to see him as something pathetic, futile and shabby, outside the great, shining stream of life towards which she was inevitably drawn.

Since his only support was that she loved him, he leaned weakly on that; the support broke, but still he held on to it and was carried out to sea and washed up on the French coast with its broken pieces still in his hands. He carried them around with him in the form of photographs and packets of correspondence and a liking for a maudlin popular song called 'Among My Souvenirs'. He kept clear of other girls, as if Caroline would somehow know it and reciprocate with a faithful heart. Her note informed him that he had lost her forever.

It was a fine morning. In front of the shops in the Rue de Castiglione, proprietors and patrons were on the sidewalk gazing upward, for the Graf Zeppelin, shining and glorious, symbol of escape and destruction – of escape, if necessary, through destruction – glided in the Paris sky. He heard a woman say in French that it would not her astonish if that commenced to let fall the bombs. Then he heard another voice, full of husky laughter, and the void in his stomach froze. Jerking about, he was face to face with Caroline Dandy and her fiancé.

'Why, Michael! Why, we were wondering where you were. I asked at the Guaranty Trust, and Morgan and Company, and finally sent a note to the National City—'

Why didn't they back away? Why didn't they back right up, walking backwards down the Rue de Castiglione, across the Rue de Rivoli, through the Tuileries Gardens, still walking backwards as fast as they could till they grew vague and faded out across the river?

'This is Hamilton Rutherford, my fiancé.'

'We've met before.'

'At Pat's, wasn't it?'

'And last spring in the Ritz Bar.'

'Michael, where have you been keeping yourself?'

'Around here.' This agony. Previews of Hamilton Rutherford flashed before his eyes – a quick series of pictures, sentences. He remembered hearing that he had bought a seat in 1920 for a hundred and twenty-five thousand of borrowed money, and just before the break sold it for more than half a million. Not handsome like Michael, but vitally attractive, confident, authoritative, just the right height over Caroline there – Michael had always been too short for Caroline when they danced.

Rutherford was saying: 'No, I'd like it very much if you'd come to the bachelor dinner. I'm taking the Ritz Bar from nine o'clock on. Then right after the wedding there'll be a reception and breakfast at the Hotel George-Cinq.'

'And, Michael, George Packman is giving a party day after tomorrow at Chez Victor, and I want you to be sure and come. And also to tea Friday at Jebby West's; she'd want to have you if she knew where you were. What's your hotel, so we can send you an invitation? You see, the reason we decided to have it over here is because mother has been sick in a nursing home here and the whole clan is in Paris. Then Hamilton's mother's being here too—'

The entire clan; they had always hated him, except her mother; always discouraged his courtship. What a little counter he was in this game of families and money! Under his hat his brow sweated with the humiliation of the fact that for all his misery he was worth just exactly so many invitations. Frantically he began to mumble something about going away.

Then it happened – Caroline saw deep into him, and Michael knew that she saw. She saw through to his profound woundedness, and something quivered inside her, died out along the curve of her mouth and in her eyes. He had moved her. All the unforgettable impulses of first love had surged up once more; their hearts had in some way touched across two feet of Paris sunlight. She took her fiancé's arm suddenly, as if to steady herself with the feel of it.

They parted. Michael walked quickly for a minute; then he stopped, pretending to look in a window, and saw them farther up the street, walking fast into the Place Vendôme, people with much to do.

He had things to do also – he had to get his laundry.

'Nothing will ever be the same again,' he said to himself. 'She will never be happy in her marriage and I will never be happy at all any more.'

The two vivid years of his love for Caroline moved back around him like years in Einstein's physics. Intolerable memories arose – of rides in the Long Island moonlight; of a happy time at Lake Placid with her cheeks so cold there, but warm just underneath the surface; of a despairing afternoon in a little café on Forty-eighth Street in the last sad months when their marriage had come to seem impossible.

'Come in,' he said aloud.

The concierge with a telegram; brusque because Mr Curly's clothes were a little shabby. Mr Curly gave few tips; Mr Curly was obviously a *petit client*.

Michael read the telegram.

'An answer?' the concierge asked.

'No,' said Michael, and then, on an impulse: 'Look.'

'Too bad – too bad,' said the concierge. 'Your grandfather is dead.'

'Not too bad,' said Michael. 'It means that I come into a quarter of a million dollars.'

Too late by a single month; after the first flush of the news his misery was deeper than ever. Lying awake in bed that night, he listened endlessly to the long caravan of a circus moving through the street from one Paris fair to another.

When the last van had rumbled out of hearing and the corners of the furniture were pastel blue with the dawn, he was still thinking of the look in Caroline's eyes that morning – the look that seemed to say: 'Oh, why couldn't you have done something about it? Why couldn't you have been stronger, made me marry you? Don't you see how sad I am?'

Michael's fists clenched.

'Well, I won't give up till the last moment,' he whispered. 'I've had all the bad luck so far, and maybe it's turned at last. One takes what one can get, up to the limit of one's strength, and if I can't have her, at least she'll go into this marriage with some of me in her heart.'

II

ACCORDINGLY HE WENT to the party at Chez Victor two days later, upstairs and into the little salon off the bar where the party was to assemble for cocktails. He was early; the only other occupant was a tall lean man of fifty. They spoke.

'You waiting for George Packman's party?'

'Yes. My name's Michael Curly.'

'My name's—'

Michael failed to catch the name. They ordered a drink, and Michael supposed that the bride and groom were having a gay time.

'Too much so,' the other agreed, frowning. 'I don't see how they stand it. We all crossed on the boat together; five days of that crazy life and then two weeks of Paris. You' – he hesitated, smiling faintly – 'you'll excuse me for saying that your generation drinks too much.'

'Not Caroline.'

'No, not Caroline. She seems to take only a cocktail and a glass of champagne, and then she's had enough, thank God. But Hamilton drinks too much and all this crowd of young people drink too much. Do you live in Paris?'

'For the moment,' said Michael.

'I don't like Paris. My wife – that is to say, my ex-wife, Hamilton's mother – lives in Paris.'

'You're Hamilton Rutherford's father?'

'I have that honour. And I'm not denying that I'm proud of what he's done; it was just a general comment.'

'Of course.'

Michael glanced up nervously as four people came in. He felt suddenly that his dinner coat was old and shiny; he had ordered a new one that morning. The people who had come in were rich and at home in their richness with one another – a dark, lovely girl with a hysterical little laugh whom he had met before; two confident men whose jokes referred invariably to last night's scandal and tonight's potentialities, as if they had important rôles in a play that extended indefinitely into the past and the future. When Caroline arrived, Michael had scarcely a moment of her, but it was enough to note that, like all the others, she was strained and tired. She was pale beneath her rouge; there were shadows under her eyes. With a mixture of relief and wounded vanity, he found himself placed far from her and at another table; he needed a moment to adjust himself to his surroundings. This was not like the immature set in which he and Caroline had moved; the men were more than thirty and had an air of sharing the best of this world's good. Next to him was Jebby West, whom he knew; and, on the other side, a jovial man who immediately began to talk to Michael about a stunt for the bachelor dinner: they were going to hire a French girl to appear with an actual baby in her arms, crying: 'Hamilton, you can't desert me now!' The idea seemed stale and unamusing to Michael, but its originator shook with anticipatory laughter.

Farther up the table there was talk of the market – another drop today, the most appreciable since the crash; people were kidding Rutherford about it: 'Too bad, old man. You better not get married, after all.'

Michael asked the man on his left, 'Has he lost a lot?'

'Nobody knows. He's heavily involved, but he's one of the smartest young men in Wall Street. Anyhow, nobody ever tells you the truth.'

It was a champagne dinner from the start, and towards the end it reached a pleasant level of conviviality, but Michael saw that all these people were too weary to be exhilarated by any ordinary stimulant; for weeks they had drunk cocktails before meals like Americans, wines and brandies like Frenchmen, beer like Germans, whisky-and-soda like the

English, and as they were no longer in the twenties, this preposterous *mélange*, that was like some gigantic cocktail in a nightmare, served only to make them temporarily less conscious of the mistakes of the night before. Which is to say that it was not really a gay party; what gaiety existed was displayed in the few who drank nothing at all.

But Michael was not tired, and the champagne stimulated him and made his misery less acute. He had been away from New York for more than eight months and most of the dance music was unfamiliar to him, but at the first bars of the 'Painted Doll' to which he and Caroline had moved through so much happiness and despair the previous summer, he crossed to Caroline's table and asked her to dance.

She was lovely in a dress of thin ethereal blue, and the proximity of her crackly yellow hair, of her cool and tender grey eyes, turned his body clumsy and rigid; he stumbled with their first step on the floor. For a moment it seemed that there was nothing to say; he wanted to tell her about his inheritance, but the idea seemed abrupt, unprepared for.

'Michael, it's so nice to be dancing with you again.'

He smiled grimly.

'I'm so happy you came,' she continued. 'I was afraid maybe you'd be silly and stay away. Now we can be just good friends and natural together. Michael, I want you and Hamilton to like each other.'

The engagement was making her stupid; he had never heard her make such a series of obvious remarks before.

'I could kill him without a qualm,' he said pleasantly, 'but he looks like a good man. He's fine. What I want to know is, what happens to people like me who aren't able to forget?'

As he said this he could not prevent his mouth from drooping suddenly, and glancing up, Caroline saw, and her heart quivered violently, as it had the other morning.

'Do you mind so much, Michael?'

'Yes.'

For a second as he said this, in a voice that seemed to have come up from his shoes, they were not dancing; they were simply clinging together. Then she leaned away from him and twisted her mouth into a lovely smile.

'I didn't know what to do at first, Michael. I told Hamilton about you – that I'd cared for you an awful lot – but it didn't worry him, and he was right. Because I'm over you now – yes, I am. And you'll wake up some sunny morning and be over me just like that.'

He shook his head stubbornly.

'Oh, yes. We weren't for each other. I'm pretty flighty, and I need somebody like Hamilton to decide things. It was that more than the question of – of—'

'Of money.' Again he was on the point of telling her what had happened, but again something told him it was not the time.

'Then how do you account for what happened when we met the other day,' he demanded helplessly – 'what happened just now? When we just pour toward each other like we used to – as if we were one person, as if the same blood was flowing through both of us?'

'Oh, don't,' she begged him. 'You mustn't talk like that; everything's decided now. I love Hamilton with all my heart. It's just that I remember certain things in the past and I feel sorry for you – for us – for the way we were.'

Over her shoulder, Michael saw a man come toward them to cut in. In a panic he danced her away, but inevitably the man came on.

'I've got to see you alone, if only for a minute,' Michael said quickly. 'When can I?'

'I'll be at Jebby West's tea tomorrow,' she whispered as a hand fell politely upon Michael's shoulder.

But he did not talk to her at Jebby West's tea. Rutherford stood next to her, and each brought the other into all conversations. They left early. The next morning the wedding cards arrived in the first mail.

Then Michael, grown desperate with pacing up and down his room, determined on a bold stroke; he wrote to Hamilton Rutherford, asking him for a rendezvous the following afternoon. In a short telephone communication Rutherford agreed, but for a day later than Michael had asked. And the wedding was only six days away.

They were to meet in the bar of the Hotel Jena. Michael knew what he would say: 'See here, Rutherford, do you realize the responsibility you're taking in going through with this marriage? Do you realize the harvest of trouble and regret you're sowing in persuading a girl into something contrary to the instincts of her heart?' He would explain that the barrier between Caroline and himself had been an artificial one and was now removed, and demand that the matter be put up to Caroline frankly before it was too late.

Rutherford would be angry, conceivably there would be a scene, but Michael felt that he was fighting for his life now.

He found Rutherford in conversation with an older man, whom Michael had met at several of the wedding parties.

'I saw what happened to most of my friends,' Rutherford was saying, 'and I decided it wasn't going to happen to me. It isn't so difficult; if you take a girl with common sense, and tell her what's what, and do your stuff damn well, and play decently square with her, it's a marriage. If you stand for any nonsense at the beginning, it's one of these arrangements – within five years the man gets out, or else the girl gobbles him up and you have the usual mess.'

'Right!' agreed his companion enthusiastically. 'Hamilton, boy, you're right.'

Michael's blood boiled slowly.

'Doesn't it strike you,' he inquired coldly, 'that your attitude went out of fashion about a hundred years ago?'

'No, it didn't,' said Rutherford pleasantly, but impatiently. 'I'm as modern as anybody. I'd get married in an aeroplane next Saturday if it'd please my girl.'

'I don't mean that way of being modern. You can't take a sensitive woman—'

'Sensitive? Women aren't so darn sensitive. It's fellows like you who are sensitive; it's fellows like you they exploit – all your devotion and kindness and all that. They read a couple of books and see a few pictures because they haven't got anything else to do, and then they say they're finer in grain than you are, and to prove it they take the bit in their teeth and tear off for a fare-you-well – just about as sensitive as a fire horse.'

'Caroline happens to be sensitive,' said Michael in a clipped voice.

At this point the other man got up to go; when the dispute about the check had been settled and they were alone, Rutherford leaned back to Michael as if a question had been asked him.

'Caroline's more than sensitive,' he said. 'She's got sense.'

His combative eyes, meeting Michael's, flickered with a grey light. 'This all sounds pretty crude to you, Mr Curly, but it seems to me that the average man nowadays just asks to be made a monkey of by some woman who doesn't even get any fun out of reducing him to that level. There are darn few men who possess their wives any more, but I am going to be one of them.'

To Michael it seemed time to bring the talk back to the actual situation: 'Do you realize the responsibility you're taking?'

'I certainly do,' interrupted Rutherford. 'I'm not afraid of responsibility. I'll make the decisions – fairly, I hope, but anyhow they'll be final.'

'What if you didn't start right?' said Michael impetuously. 'What if your marriage isn't founded on mutual love?'

'I think I see what you mean,' Rutherford said, still pleasant. 'And since you've brought it up, let me say that if you and Caroline had married, it wouldn't have lasted three years. Do you know what your affair was founded on? On sorrow. You got sorry for each other. Sorrow's a lot of fun for most women and for some men, but it seems to me that a marriage ought to be based on hope.' He looked at his watch and stood up.

'I've got to meet Caroline. Remember, you're coming to the bachelor dinner day after tomorrow.'

Michael felt the moment slipping away. 'Then Caroline's personal feelings don't count with you?' he demanded fiercely.

'Caroline's tired and upset. But she has what she wants, and that's the main thing.'

'Are you referring to yourself?' demanded Michael incredulously.

'Yes.'

'May I ask how long she's wanted you?'

'About two years.' Before Michael could answer, he was gone.

During the next two days Michael floated in an abyss of helplessness. The idea haunted him that he had left something undone that would sever this knot drawn tighter under his eyes. He phoned Caroline, but she insisted that it was physically impossible for her to see him until the day before the wedding, for which day she granted him a tentative rendezvous. Then he went to the bachelor dinner, partly in fear of an evening alone at his hotel, partly from a feeling that by his presence at that function he was somehow nearer to Caroline, keeping her in sight.

The Ritz Bar had been prepared for the occasion by French and American banners and by a great canvas covering one wall, against which the guests were invited to concentrate their proclivities in breaking glasses.

At the first cocktail, taken at the bar, there were many slight spillings from many trembling hands, but later, with the champagne, there was a rising tide of laughter and occasional bursts of song.

Michael was surprised to find what a difference his new dinner coat, his new silk hat, his new, proud linen made in his estimate of himself; he felt less resentment towards all these people for being so rich and assured. For the first time since he had left college he felt rich and assured himself; he felt that he was part of all this, and even entered into the scheme of Johnson, the practical joker, for the appearance of the woman betrayed, now waiting tranquilly in the room across the hall.

'We don't want to go too heavy,' Johnson said, 'because I imagine Ham's had a pretty anxious day already. Did you see Fullman Oil's sixteen points off this morning?'

'Will that matter to him?' Michael asked, trying to keep the interest out of his voice.

'Naturally. He's in heavily; he's always in everything heavily. So far he's had luck; anyhow, up to a month ago.'

The glasses were filled and emptied faster now, and men were shouting at one another across the narrow table. Against the bar a group of ushers was being photographed, and the flash light surged through the room in a stifling cloud.

'Now's the time,' Johnson said. 'You're to stand by the door, remember, and we're both to try and keep her from coming in – just till we get everybody's attention.'

He went on out into the corridor, and Michael waited obediently by the door. Several minutes passed. Then Johnson reappeared with a curious expression on his face.

'There's something funny about this.'

'Isn't the girl there?'

'She's there all right, but there's another woman there, too; and it's nobody we engaged either. She wants to see Hamilton Rutherford, and she looks as if she had something on her mind.'

They went out into the hall. Planted firmly in a chair near the door sat an American girl a little the worse for liquor, but with a determined expression on her face. She looked up at them with a jerk of her head.

'Well, j'tell him?' she demanded. 'The name is Marjorie Collins, and he'll know it. I've come a long way, and I want to see him now and quick, or there's going to be more trouble than you ever saw.' She rose unsteadily to her feet.

'You go in and tell Ham,' whispered Johnson to Michael. 'Maybe he'd better get out. I'll keep her here.'

Back at the table, Michael leaned close to Rutherford's ear and, with a certain grimness, whispered:

'A girl outside named Marjorie Collins says she wants to see you. She looks as if she wanted to make trouble.'

Hamilton Rutherford blinked and his mouth fell ajar; then slowly the lips came together in a straight line and he said in a crisp voice:

'Please keep her there. And send the head barman to me right away.'

Michael spoke to the barman, and then, without returning to the table, asked quietly for his coat and hat. Out in the hall again, he passed Johnson and the girl without speaking and went out into the Rue Cambon. Calling a cab, he gave the address of Caroline's hotel.

His place was beside her now. Not to bring bad news, but simply to be with her when her house of cards came falling around her head.

Rutherford had implied that he was soft – well, he was hard enough not to give up the girl he loved without taking advantage of every chance within the pale of honour. Should she turn away from Rutherford, she would find him there.

She was in; she was surprised when he called, but she was still dressed and would be down immediately. Presently she appeared in a dinner gown, holding two blue telegrams in her hand. They sat down in armchairs in the deserted lobby.

'But, Michael, is the dinner over?'

'I wanted to see you, so I came away.'

'I'm glad.' Her voice was friendly, but matter-of-fact. 'Because I'd just phoned your hotel that I had fittings and rehearsals all day tomorrow. Now we can have our talk after all.'

'You're tired,' he guessed. 'Perhaps I shouldn't have come.'

'No. I was waiting up for Hamilton. Telegrams that may be important. He said he might go on somewhere, and that may mean any hour, so I'm glad I have someone to talk to.'

Michael winced at the impersonality in the last phrase.

'Don't you care when he gets home?'

'Naturally,' she said, laughing, 'but I haven't got much say about it, have I?'

'Why not?'

'I couldn't start by telling him what he could and couldn't do.'

'Why not?'

'He wouldn't stand for it.'

'He seems to want merely a housekeeper,' said Michael ironically.

'Tell me about your plans, Michael,' she asked quickly.

'My plans? I can't see any future after the day after tomorrow. The only real plan I ever had was to love you.'

Their eyes brushed past each other's, and the look he knew so well was staring out at him from hers. Words flowed quickly from his heart:

'Let me tell you just once more how well I've loved you, never wavering for a moment, never thinking of another girl. And now when I think of all the years ahead without you, without any hope, I don't want to live, Caroline darling. I used to dream about our home, our children, about holding you in my arms and touching your face and hands and hair that used to belong to me, and now I just can't wake up.'

Caroline was crying softly. 'Poor Michael – poor Michael.' Her hand reached out and her fingers brushed the lapel of his dinner coat. 'I was so sorry for you the other night. You looked so thin, and as if you needed a new suit and somebody to take care of you.' She sniffled and looked more closely at his coat. 'Why, you've got a new suit! And a new silk hat! Why, Michael, how swell!' She laughed, suddenly cheerful through her tears. 'You must have come into money, Michael; I never saw you so well turned out.'

For a moment, at her reaction, he hated his new clothes.

'I have come into money,' he said. 'My grandfather left me about a quarter of a million dollars.'

'Why, Michael,' she cried, 'how perfectly swell! I can't tell you how glad I am. I've always thought you were the sort of person who ought to have money.'

'Yes, just too late to make a difference.'

The revolving door from the street groaned around and Hamilton Rutherford came into the lobby. His face was flushed, his eyes were restless and impatient.

'Hello, darling; hello, Mr Curly.' He bent and kissed Caroline. 'I broke away for a minute to find out if I had any telegrams. I see you've got them there.' Taking them from her, he remarked to Curly, 'That was an odd business there in the bar, wasn't it? Especially as I understand some of you had a joke fixed up in the same line.' He opened one of the telegrams, closed it and turned to Caroline with the divided expression of a man carrying two things in his head at once.

'A girl I haven't seen for two years turned up,' he said. 'It seemed to be some clumsy form of blackmail, for I haven't and never have had any sort of obligation towards her whatever.'

'What happened?'

'The head barman had a Sûreté Générale man there in ten minutes and it was settled in the hall. The French blackmail laws make ours look like a sweet wish, and I gather they threw a scare into her that she'll remember. But it seems wiser to tell you.'

'Are you implying that I mentioned the matter?' said Michael stiffly.

'No,' Rutherford said slowly. 'No, you were just going to be on hand. And since you're here, I'll tell you some news that will interest you even more.'

He handed Michael one telegram and opened the other.

'This is in code,' Michael said.

'So is this. But I've got to know all the words pretty well this last week. The two of them together mean that I'm due to start life all over.'

Michael saw Caroline's face grow a shade paler, but she sat quiet as a mouse.

'It was a mistake and I stuck to it too long,' continued Rutherford. 'So you see I don't have all the luck, Mr Curly. By the way, they tell me you've come into money.'

'Yes,' said Michael.

'There we are, then.' Rutherford turned to Caroline. 'You understand, darling, that I'm not joking or exaggerating. I've lost almost every cent I had and I'm starting life over.'

Two pairs of eyes were regarding her – Rutherford's noncommittal and unrequiring, Michael's hungry, tragic, pleading. In a minute she had raised herself from the chair and with a little cry thrown herself into Hamilton Rutherford's arms.

'Oh, darling,' she cried, 'what does it matter! It's

better; I like it better, honestly I do! I want to start that way; I want to! Oh, please don't worry or be sad even for a minute!'

'All right, baby,' said Rutherford. His hand stroked her hair gently for a moment; then he took his arm from around her.

'I promised to join the party for an hour,' he said. 'So I'll say good night, and I want you to go to bed soon and get a good sleep. Good night, Mr Curly. I'm sorry to have let you in for all these financial matters.'

But Michael had already picked up his hat and cane. 'I'll go along with you,' he said.

III

IT WAS SUCH a fine morning. Michael's cutaway hadn't been delivered, so he felt rather uncomfortable passing before the cameras and moving-picture machines in front of the little church on the Avenue George-Cinq.

It was such a clean, new church that it seemed unforgivable not to be dressed properly, and Michael, white and shaky after a sleepless night, decided to stand in the rear. From there he looked at the back of Hamilton Rutherford, and the lacy, filmy back of Caroline, and the fat back of George Packman, which looked unsteady, as if it wanted to lean against the bride and groom.

The ceremony went on for a long time under the gay flags and pennons overhead, under the thick beams of June sunlight slanting down through the tall windows upon the well-dressed people.

As the procession, headed by the bride and groom, started down the aisle, Michael realized with alarm he was just where everyone would dispense with their parade stiffness, become informal and speak to him.

So it turned out. Rutherford and Caroline spoke first to him; Rutherford grim with the strain of being married, and Caroline lovelier than he had ever seen her, floating all softly down through the friends and relatives of her youth, down through the past and forward to the future by the sunlit door.

Michael managed to murmur, 'Beautiful, simply beautiful,' and then other people passed and spoke to him – old Mrs Dandy, straight from her sickbed and looking remarkably well, or carrying it off like the very fine old lady she was; and Rutherford's father and mother, ten years divorced, but walking side by side and looking made for each other and proud. Then all Caroline's sisters and their husbands and her little nephews in Eton suits, and then a long parade, all speaking to Michael because he was still standing paralyzed just at that point where the procession broke.

He wondered what would happen now. Cards had

been issued for a reception at the George-Cinq; an expensive enough place, heaven knew. Would Rutherford try to go through with that on top of those disastrous telegrams? Evidently, for the procession outside was streaming up there through the June morning, three by three and four by four. On the corner the long dresses of girls, five abreast, fluttered many-coloured in the wind. Girls had become gossamer again, perambulatory flora; such lovely fluttering dresses in the bright noon wind.

Michael needed a drink; he couldn't face that reception line without a drink. Diving into a side doorway of the hotel, he asked for the bar, whither a *chasseur* led him through half a kilometre of new American-looking passages.

But – how did it happen? – the bar was full. There were ten – fifteen men and two – four girls, all from the wedding, all needing a drink. There were cocktails and champagne in the bar; Rutherford's cocktails and champagne, as it turned out, for he had engaged the whole bar and the ballroom and the two great reception rooms and all the stairways leading up and down, and windows looking out over the whole square block of Paris. By and by Michael went and joined the long, slow drift of the receiving line. Through a flowery mist of 'Such a lovely wedding', 'My dear, you were simply lovely', 'You're a lucky man, Rutherford' he passed down the line. When Michael came to Caroline, she took a single step forward and kissed him on the lips, but he felt no contact in the kiss; it was unreal and he floated on away from it. Old Mrs Dandy, who had always liked him, held his hand for a minute and thanked him for the flowers he had sent when he heard she was ill.

'I'm so sorry not to have written; you know, we old ladies are grateful for—' The flowers, the fact that she had not written, the wedding – Michael saw that they all had the same relative importance to her now; she had married off five other children and seen two of the marriages go to pieces, and this scene, so poignant, so confusing to Michael, appeared to her simply a familiar charade in which she had played her part before.

A buffet luncheon with champagne was already being served at small tables and there was an orchestra playing in the empty ballroom. Michael sat down with Jebby West; he was still a little embarrassed at not wearing a morning coat, but he perceived now that he was not alone in the omission and felt better. 'Wasn't Caroline divine?' Jebby West said. 'So entirely self-possessed. I asked her this morning if she wasn't a little nervous at stepping off like this. And she said, "Why should I be? I've been after him for two years, and now I'm just happy, that's all."'

'It must be true,' said Michael gloomily.

'What?'

'What you just said.'

He had been stabbed, but, rather to his distress, he did not feel the wound.

He asked Jebby to dance. Out on the floor, Rutherford's father and mother were dancing together.

'It makes me a little sad, that,' she said. 'Those two hadn't met for years; both of them were married again and she divorced again. She went to the station to meet him when he came over for Caroline's wedding, and invited him to stay at her house in the Avenue du Bois with a whole lot of other people, perfectly proper, but he was afraid his wife would hear about it and not like it, so he went to a hotel. Don't you think that's sort of sad?'

An hour or so later Michael realized suddenly that it was afternoon. In one corner of the ballroom an arrangement of screens like a moving-picture stage had been set up and photographers were taking official pictures of the bridal party. The bridal party, still as death and pale as wax under the bright lights, appeared, to the dancers circling the modulated semi-darkness of the ballroom, like those jovial or sinister groups that one comes upon in The Old Mill at an amusement park.

After the bridal party had been photographed, there was a group of the ushers; then the bridesmaids, the families, the children. Later, Caroline, active and excited, having long since abandoned the repose implicit in her flowing dress and great bouquet, came and plucked Michael off the floor.

'Now we'll have them take one of just old friends.' Her voice implied that this was best, most intimate of all. 'Come here, Jebby, George – not you, Hamilton; this is just my friends – Sally—'

A little after that, what remained of formality disappeared and the hours flowed easily down the profuse stream of champagne. In the modern fashion, Hamilton Rutherford sat at the table with his arm about an old girl of his and assured his guests, which included not a few bewildered but enthusiastic Europeans, that the party was not nearly at an end; it was to reassemble at Zelli's after midnight. Michael saw Mrs Dandy, not quite over her illness, rise to go and become caught in polite group after group, and he spoke of it to one of her daughters, who thereupon forcibly abducted her mother and called her car. Michael felt very considerate and proud of himself after having done this, and drank much more champagne.

'It's amazing,' George Packman was telling him enthusiastically. 'This show will cost Ham about five thousand dollars, and I understand they'll be just about his last. But did he countermand a bottle of champagne or a flower? Not he! He happens to have it – that young man. Do you know that T. G. Vance offered him a salary of fifty thousand dollars a year ten minutes before the wedding this morning? In another year he'll be back with the millionaires.'

The conversation was interrupted by a plan to carry Rutherford out on communal shoulders – a plan which six of them put into effect, and then stood in the four-o'clock sunshine waving good-bye to the bride and groom. But there must have been a mistake somewhere, for five minutes later Michael saw both bride and groom descending the stairway to the reception, each with a glass of champagne held defiantly on high.

'This is our way of doing things,' he thought. 'Generous and fresh and free; a sort of Virginia-plantation hospitality, but at a different pace now, nervous as a ticker tape.'

Standing unselfconsciously in the middle of the room to see which was the American ambassador, he realized with a start that he hadn't really thought of Caroline for hours. He looked about him with a sort of alarm, and then he saw her across the room, very bright and young, and radiantly happy. He saw Rutherford near her, looking at her as if he could never look long enough, and as Michael watched them they seemed to recede as he had wished them to do that day in the Rue de Castiglione – recede and fade off into joys and griefs of their own, into the years that would take the toll of Rutherford's fine pride and Caroline's young, moving beauty; fade far away, so that now he could scarcely see them, as if they were shrouded in something as misty as her white, billowing dress.

Michael was cured. The ceremonial function, with its pomp and its revelry, had stood for a sort of initiation into a life where even his regret could not follow them. All the bitterness melted out of him suddenly and the world reconstituted itself out of the youth and happiness that was all around him, profligate as the spring sunshine. He was trying to remember which one of the bridesmaids he had made a date to dine with tonight as he walked forward to bid Hamilton and Caroline Rutherford good-bye.

5

The Baby Party

When John Andros felt old he found solace in the thought of life continuing through his child. The dark trumpets of oblivion were less loud at the patter of his child's feet or at the sound of his child's voice babbling mad non sequiturs to him over the telephone. The latter incident occurred every afternoon at three when his wife called the office from the country, and he came to look forward to it as one of the vivid minutes of his day.

He was not physically old, but his life had been a series of struggles up a series of rugged hills, and here at thirty-eight having won his battles against ill-health and poverty he cherished less than the usual number of illusions. Even his feeling about his little girl was qualified. She had interrupted his rather intense love-affair with his wife, and she was the reason for their living in a suburban town, where they paid for country air with endless servant troubles and the weary merry-go-round of the commuting train.

It was little Ede as a definite piece of youth that chiefly interested him. He liked to take her on his lap and examine minutely her fragrant, downy scalp and her eyes with their irises of morning blue. Having paid this homage John was content that the nurse should take her away. After ten minutes the very vitality of the child irritated him; he was inclined to lose his temper when things were broken, and one Sunday afternoon when she had disrupted a bridge game by permanently hiding up the ace of spades, he had made a scene that had reduced his wife to tears.

This was absurd and John was ashamed of himself. It was inevitable that such things would happen, and it was impossible that little Ede should spend all her indoor hours in the nursery upstairs when she was becoming, as her mother said, more nearly a 'real person' every day.

She was two and a half, and this afternoon, for instance, she was going to a baby party. Grown-up Edith, her mother, had telephoned the information to the office, and little Ede had confirmed the business by shouting 'I yam going to a *pantry*!' into John's unsuspecting left ear.

'Drop in at the Markeys' when you get home, won't

you, dear?' resumed her mother. 'It'll be funny. Ede's going to be all dressed up in her new pink dress—'

The conversation terminated abruptly with a squawk which indicated that the telephone had been pulled violently to the floor. John laughed and decided to get an early train out; the prospect of a baby party in someone else's house amused him.

'What a peach of a mess!' he thought humorously. 'A dozen mothers, and each one looking at nothing but her own child. All the babies breaking things and grabbing at the cake, and each mama going home thinking about the subtle superiority of her own child to every other child there.'

He was in a good humour today – all the things in his life were going better than they had ever gone before. When he got off the train at his station he shook his head at an importunate taxi man, and began to walk up the long hill towards his house through the crisp December twilight. It was only six o'clock but the moon was out, shining with proud brilliance on the thin sugary snow that lay over the lawns.

As he walked along drawing his lungs full of cold air his happiness increased, and the idea of a baby party appealed to him more and more. He began to wonder how Ede compared to other children of her own age, and if the pink dress she was to wear was something radical and mature. Increasing his gait he came in sight of his own house, where the lights of a defunct Christmas-tree still blossomed in the window, but he continued on past the walk. The party was at the Markeys' next door.

As he mounted the brick step and rang the bell he became aware of voices inside, and he was glad he was not too late. Then he raised his head and listened – the voices were not children's voices, but they were loud and pitched high with anger; there were at least three of them and one, which rose as he listened to a hysterical sob, he recognized immediately as his wife's.

'There's been some trouble,' he thought quickly.

Trying the door, he found it unlocked and pushed it open.

The baby party started at half past four, but Edith Andros, calculating shrewdly that the new dress would stand out more sensationally against vestments already rumpled, planned the arrival of herself and little Ede for five. When they appeared it was already a flourishing affair. Four baby girls and nine baby boys, each one curled and washed and dressed with all the care of a proud and jealous heart, were dancing to the music of a phonograph. Never more than two or three were dancing at once, but as all were continually in motion running to and from their mothers for encouragement, the general effect was the same.

As Edith and her daughter entered, the music was temporarily drowned out by a sustained chorus, consisting largely of the word cute and directed towards little Ede, who stood looking timidly about and fingering the edges of her pink dress. She was not kissed – this is the sanitary age – but she was passed along a row of mamas each one of whom said 'cu-u-ute' to her and held her pink little hand before passing her on to the next. After some encouragement and a few mild pushes she was absorbed into the dance, and became an active member of the party.

Edith stood near the door talking to Mrs Markey, and keeping an eye on the tiny figure in the pink dress. She did not care for Mrs Markey; she considered her both snippy and common, but John and Joe Markey were congenial and went in together on the commuting train every morning, so the two women kept up an elaborate pretence of warm amity. They were always reproaching each other for 'not coming to see me', and they were always planning the kind of parties that began with 'You'll have to come to dinner with us soon, and we'll go to the theatre,' but never matured further.

'Little Ede looks perfectly darling,' said Mrs Markey, smiling and moistening her lips in a way that Edith found particularly repulsive. 'So *grown-up* – I can't *believe* it!'

Edith wondered if 'little Ede' referred to the fact

that Billy Markey, though several months younger, weighed almost five pounds more. Accepting a cup of tea she took a seat with two other ladies on a divan and launched into the real business of the afternoon, which of course lay in relating the recent accomplishments and insouciances of her child.

An hour passed. Dancing palled and the babies took to sterner sport. They ran into the dining-room, rounded the big table, and essayed the kitchen door, from which they were rescued by an expeditionary force of mothers. Having been rounded up they immediately broke loose, and rushing back to the dining-room tried the familiar swinging door again. The word 'overheated' began to be used, and small white brows were dried with small white handkerchiefs. A general attempt to make the babies sit down began, but the babies squirmed off laps with peremptory cries of 'Down! Down!' and the rush into the fascinating dining-room began anew.

This phase of the party came to an end with the arrival of refreshments, a large cake with two candles, and saucers of vanilla ice-cream. Billy Markey, a stout laughing baby with red hair and legs somewhat bowed, blew out the candles, and placed an experimental thumb on the white frosting. The refreshments were distributed, and the children ate, greedily but without confusion – they had behaved remarkably well all afternoon. They were modern babies who ate and slept at regular hours, so their dispositions were good, and their faces healthy and pink – such a peaceful party would not have been possible thirty years ago.

After the refreshments a gradual exodus began. Edith glanced anxiously at her watch – it was almost six, and John had not arrived. She wanted him to see Ede with the other children – to see how dignified and polite and intelligent she was, and how the only ice-cream spot on her dress was some that had dropped from her chin when she was joggled from behind.

'You're a darling,' she whispered to her child, drawing her suddenly against her knee. 'Do you know you're a darling? Do you know you're a darling?'

Ede laughed. 'Bow-wow,' she said suddenly.

'Bow-wow?' Edith looked around. 'There isn't any bow-wow.'

'Bow-wow,' repeated Ede. 'I want a bow-wow.'

Edith followed the small pointing finger.

'That isn't a bow-wow, dearest, that's a teddy-bear.'

'Bear?'

'Yes, that's a teddy-bear, and it belongs to Billy Markey. You don't want Billy Markey's teddy-bear, do you?'

Ede did want it.

She broke away from her mother and approached

Billy Markey, who held the toy closely in his arms. Ede stood regarding him with inscrutable eyes, and Billy laughed.

Grown-up Edith looked at her watch again, this time impatiently.

The party had dwindled until, besides Ede and Billy, there were only two babies remaining – and one of the two remained only by virtue of having hidden himself under the dining-room table. It was selfish of John not to come. It showed so little pride in the child. Other fathers had come, half a dozen of them, to call for their wives, and they had stayed for a while and looked on.

There was a sudden wail. Ede had obtained Billy's teddy-bear by pulling it forcibly from his arms, and on Billy's attempt to recover it, she had pushed him casually to the floor.

'Why, Ede!' cried her mother, repressing an inclination to laugh.

Joe Markey, a handsome, broad-shouldered man of thirty-five, picked up his son and set him on his feet. 'You're a fine fellow,' he said jovially. 'Let a girl knock you over! You're a fine fellow.'

'Did he bump his head?' Mrs Markey returned anxiously from bowing the next to last remaining mother out of the door.

'No-o-o-o,' exclaimed Markey. 'He bumped

something else, didn't you, Billy? He bumped something else.'

Billy had so far forgotten the bump that he was already making an attempt to recover his property. He seized a leg of the bear which projected from Ede's enveloping arms and tugged at it but without success.

'No,' said Ede emphatically.

Suddenly, encouraged by the success of her former half-accidental manoeuvre, Ede dropped the teddy-bear, placed her hands on Billy's shoulders and pushed him backward off his feet.

This time he landed less harmlessly; his head hit the bare floor just off the rug with a dull hollow sound, whereupon he drew in his breath and delivered an agonized yell.

Immediately the room was in confusion. With an exclamation Markey hurried to his son, but his wife was first to reach the injured baby and catch him up into her arms.

'Oh, *Billy*,' she cried, 'what a terrible bump! She ought to be spanked.'

Edith, who had rushed immediately to her daughter, heard this remark, and her lips came sharply together.

'Why, Ede,' she whispered perfunctorily, 'you bad girl!'

Ede put back her little head suddenly and laughed. It was a loud laugh, a triumphant laugh with victory in it and challenge and contempt. Unfortunately it was also an infectious laugh. Before her mother realized the delicacy of the situation, she too had laughed, an audible, distinct laugh not unlike the baby's, and partaking of the same overtones.

Then, as suddenly, she stopped.

Mrs Markey's face had grown red with anger, and Markey, who had been feeling the back of the baby's head with one finger, looked at her, frowning.

'It's swollen already,' he said with a note of reproof in his voice. 'I'll get some witch-hazel.'

But Mrs Markey had lost her temper. 'I don't see anything funny about a child being hurt!' she said in a trembling voice.

Little Ede meanwhile had been looking at her mother curiously. She noted that her own laugh had produced her mother's and she wondered if the same cause would always produce the same effect. So she chose this moment to throw back her head and laugh again.

To her mother the additional mirth added the final touch of hysteria to the situation. Pressing her handkerchief to her mouth she giggled irrepressibly. It was more than nervousness – she felt that in a peculiar way she was laughing with her child – they were laughing together.

It was in a way a defiance – those two against the world.

While Markey rushed upstairs to the bathroom for ointment, his wife was walking up and down rocking the yelling boy in her arms.

'Please go home!' she broke out suddenly. 'The child's badly hurt, and if you haven't the decency to be quiet, you'd better go home.'

'Very well,' said Edith, her own temper rising. 'I've never seen anyone make such a mountain out of—'

'Get out!' cried Mrs Markey frantically. 'There's the door, get out – I never want to see you in our house again. You or your brat either!'

Edith had taken her daughter's hand and was moving quickly towards the door, but at this remark she stopped and turned around, her face contracting with indignation.

'Don't you dare call her that!'

Mrs Markey did not answer but continued walking up and down, muttering to herself and to Billy in an inaudible voice.

Edith began to cry.

'I will get out!' she sobbed. 'I've never heard anybody so rude and c-common in my life. I'm glad your baby did get pushed down – he's nothing but a f-fat little fool anyhow.'

Joe Markey reached the foot of the stairs just in time to hear this remark.

'Why, Mrs Andros,' he said sharply, 'can't you see the child's hurt. You really ought to control yourself.'

'Control m-myself!' exclaimed Edith brokenly. 'You better ask her to c-control herself. I've never heard anybody so c-common in my life.'

'She's insulting me!' Mrs Markey was now livid with rage. 'Did you hear what she said, Joe? I wish you'd put her out. If she won't go, just take her by the shoulders and put her out!'

'Don't you dare touch me!' cried Edith. 'I'm going just as quick as I can find my c-coat!'

Blind with tears she took a step towards the hall. It was just at this moment that the door opened and John Andros walked anxiously in.

'John!' cried Edith, and fled to him wildly.

'What's the matter? Why, what's the matter?'

'They're – they're putting me out!' she wailed, collapsing against him. 'He'd just started to take me by the shoulders and put me out. I want my coat!'

'That's not true,' objected Markey hurriedly. 'Nobody's going to put you out.' He turned to John. 'Nobody's going to put her out,' he repeated. 'She's—'

'What do you mean "put her out"?' demanded John abruptly. 'What's all this talk, anyhow?'

'Oh, let's go!' cried Edith. 'I want to go. They're so *common*, John!'

'Look here!' Markey's face darkened. 'You've said that about enough. You're acting sort of crazy.'

'They called Ede a brat!'

For the second time that afternoon little Ede

expressed emotion at an inopportune moment. Confused and frightened at the shouting voices, she began to cry, and her tears had the effect of conveying that she felt the insult in her heart.

'What's the idea of this?' broke out John. 'Do you insult your guests in your own house?'

'It seems to me it's your wife that's done the insulting!' answered Markey crisply. 'In fact, your baby there started all the trouble.'

John gave a contemptuous snort. 'Are you calling names at a little baby?' he inquired. 'That's a fine manly business!'

'Don't talk to him, John,' insisted Edith. 'Find my coat!'

'You must be in a bad way,' went on John angrily, 'if you have to take out your temper on a helpless little baby.'

'I never heard anything so damn twisted in my life,' shouted Markey. 'If that wife of yours would shut her mouth for a minute—'

'Wait a minute! You're not talking to a woman and child now—'

There was an incidental interruption. Edith had been fumbling on a chair for her coat, and Mrs Markey had been watching her with hot, angry eyes. Suddenly she laid Billy down on the sofa, where he immediately stopped crying and pulled himself upright, and coming into the hall she quickly found

Edith's coat and handed it to her without a word. Then she went back to the sofa, picked up Billy, and rocking him in her arms looked again at Edith with hot, angry eyes. The interruption had taken less than half a minute.

'Your wife comes in here and begins shouting around about how common we are!' burst out Markey violently. 'Well, if we're so damn common, you'd better stay away! And what's more, you'd better get out now!'

Again John gave a short, contemptuous laugh.

'You're not only common,' he returned, 'you're evidently an awful bully – when there's any helpless women and children around.' He felt for the knob and swung the door open. 'Come on, Edith.'

Taking up her daughter in her arms, his wife stepped outside and John, still looking contemptuously at Markey, started to follow.

'Wait a minute!' Markey took a step forward; he was trembling slightly, and two large veins on his temples were suddenly full of blood. 'You don't think you can get away with that, do you? With me?'

Without a word John walked out the door, leaving it open.

Edith, still weeping, had started for home. After following her with his eyes until she reached her own walk, John turned back towards the lighted doorway where Markey was slowly coming down the slippery steps. He took off his overcoat and hat, tossed them off the path onto the snow. Then, sliding a little on the iced walk, he took a step forward.

At the first blow, they both slipped and fell heavily to the sidewalk, half rising then, and again pulled each other to the ground. They found a better foothold in the thin snow to the side of the walk and rushed at each other, both swinging wildly and pressing out the snow into a pasty mud underfoot.

The street was deserted, and except for their short tired gasps and the padded sound as one or the other slipped down into the slushy mud, they fought in silence, clearly defined to each other by the full moonlight as well as by the amber glow that shone out of the open door. Several times they both slipped down together, and then for a while the conflict threshed about wildly on the lawn.

For ten, fifteen, twenty minutes they fought there senselessly in the moonlight. They had both taken off coats and vests at some silently agreed upon interval and now their shirts dripped from their backs in wet pulpy shreds. Both were torn and bleeding and so exhausted that they could stand only when by their position they mutually supported each other – the impact, the mere effort of a blow, would send them both to their hands and knees.

But it was not weariness that ended the business, and the very meaninglessness of the fight was a reason for not stopping. They stopped because once when they were straining at each other on the ground, they heard a man's footsteps coming along the sidewalk. They had rolled somehow into the shadow, and when they heard these footsteps they stopped fighting, stopped moving, stopped breathing, lay huddled together like two boys playing Indian until the footsteps had passed. Then, staggering to their feet, they looked at each other like two drunken men.

'I'll be damned if I'm going on with this thing any more,' cried Markey thickly.

'I'm not going on any more, either,' said John Andros. 'I've had enough of this thing.'

Again they looked at each other, sulkily this time, as if each suspected the other of urging him to a renewal of the fight. Markey spat out a mouthful of blood from a cut lip; then he cursed softly, and picking up his coat and vest, shook off the snow from them in a surprised way, as if their comparative dampness was his only worry in the world.

'Want to come in and wash up?' he asked suddenly.

'No, thanks,' said John. 'I ought to be going home – my wife'll be worried.'

He too picked up his coat and vest and then his overcoat and hat. Soaking wet and dripping with perspiration, it seemed absurd that less than half an hour ago he had been wearing all these clothes.

'Well – good night,' he said hesitantly.

Suddenly they walked towards each other and shook hands. It was no perfunctory hand-shake: John Andros's arm went around Markey's shoulder, and he patted him softly on the back for a little while.

'No harm done,' he said brokenly.

'No – you?'

'No, no harm done.'

'Well,' said John Andros after a minute, 'I guess I'll say good night.'

Limping slightly and with his clothes over his arm, John Andros turned away. The moonlight was still bright as he left the dark patch of trampled ground and walked over the intervening lawn. Down at the station, half a mile away, he could hear the rumble of the seven o'clock train.

'But you must have been crazy,' cried Edith brokenly. 'I thought you were going to fix it all up there and shake hands. That's why I went away.'

'Did you want us to fix it up?'

'Of course not, I never want to see them again. But I thought of course that was what you were going to do.' She was touching the bruises on his neck and back with iodine as he sat placidly in a hot bath. 'I'm going to get the doctor,' she said insistently. 'You may be hurt internally.'

He shook his head. 'Not a chance,' he answered. 'I don't want this to get all over the town.'

'I don't understand yet how it all happened.'

'Neither do I.' He smiled grimly. 'I guess these baby parties are pretty rough affairs.'

'Well, one thing –' suggested Edith hopefully, 'I'm certainly glad we have beef steak in the house for tomorrow's dinner.'

'Why?'

'For your eye, of course. Do you know I came within an ace of ordering veal? Wasn't that the luckiest thing?'

Half an hour later, dressed except that his neck would accommodate no collar, John moved his limbs experimentally before the glass. 'I believe I'll get myself in better shape,' he said thoughtfully. 'I must be getting old.'

'You mean so that next time you can beat him?'

'I did beat him,' he announced. 'At least, I beat him as much as he beat me. And there isn't going to be any next time. Don't you go calling people common any more. If you get in any trouble, you just take your coat and go home. Understand?'

'Yes, dear,' she said meekly. 'I was very foolish and now I understand.'

Out in the hall, he paused abruptly by the baby's door.

'Is she asleep?'

'Sound asleep. But you can go in and peek at her – just to say good night.'

They tiptoed in and bent together over the bed. Little Ede, her cheeks flushed with health, her pink hands clasped tight together, was sleeping soundly in the cool, dark room. John reached over the railing of the bed and passed his hand lightly over the silken hair.

'She's asleep,' he murmured in a puzzled way.

'Naturally, after such an afternoon.'

'Miz Andros,' the coloured maid's stage whisper floated in from the hall. 'Mr and Miz Markey down-stairs an' want to see you. Mr Markey he's all cut up in pieces, mam'n. His face look like a roast beef. An' Miz Markey she 'pear mighty mad.'

'Why, what incomparable nerve!' exclaimed Edith. 'Just tell them we're not home. I wouldn't go down for anything in the world.'

'You most certainly will.' John's voice was hard and set.

'What?'

'You'll go down right now, and, what's more, what-ever that other woman does, you'll apologize for what you said this afternoon. After that you don't ever have to see her again.'

'Why – John, I can't.'

'You've got to. And just remember that she

probably hated to come over here twice as much as you hate to go downstairs.'

'Aren't you coming? Do I have to go alone?'

'I'll be down – in just a minute.'

John Andros waited until she had closed the door behind her; then he reached over into the bed, and picking up his daughter, blankets and all, sat down in the rocking-chair holding her tightly in his arms. She moved a little, and he held his breath, but she was sleeping soundly, and in a moment she was resting quietly in the hollow of his elbow. Slowly he bent his head until his cheek was against her bright hair. 'Dear little girl,' he whispered. 'Dear little girl, dear little girl.'

John Andros knew at length what it was he had fought for so savagely that evening. He had it now, he possessed it forever, and for some time he sat there rocking very slowly to and fro in the darkness.

FRANCIS SCOTT KEY FITZGERALD was born in Minnesota in 1896. He left Princeton without graduating and joined the army in 1917. While stationed in Alabama he met Zelda Sayre and following his discharge from the army and the successful publication of his first novel *This Side of Paradise*, the pair married and later had a daughter, Frances Scott Fitzgerald. The couple's youth, beauty and notorious lifestyle made them famous during the era that Fitzgerald dubbed 'the Jazz Age'. He wrote three more novels, *The Beautiful and Damned*, *The Great Gatsby* and *Tender is the Night*, as well as volumes of short stories and *The Crack-Up*, a selection of autobiographical pieces. Fitzgerald was working on a final novel *The Last Tycoon* when he died of a heart attack in 1940, aged 44.

RECOMMENDED BOOKS BY F. SCOTT FITZGERALD:

The Beautiful and Damned
This Side of Paradise
Flappers and Philosophers

THE GREAT GATSBY

Jay Gatsby is a self-made man, famed for his decadent champagne-drenched parties. Despite being surrounded by Long Island's bright and beautiful, he longs only for Daisy Buchanan. In shimmering prose, Fitzgerald shows Gatsby pursue his dream to its tragic conclusion in one of the 20th century's true contenders for the title of 'Great American Novel'.

'*The Great Gatsby* remains not just one of the greatest works of American literature, but a timeless evocation of the allure, corruption and carelessness of wealth . . . a gilded society intoxicated by wealth, dancing its way into the Great Depression'
The Times

'A marvellously suggestive novel . . . a parable of modern America, and by extension of modern life'
Daily Telegraph

VINTAGE MINIS

The Vintage Minis bring you the world's greatest writers on the experiences that make us human. These stylish, entertaining little books explore the whole spectrum of life – from birth to death, and everything in between. Which means there's something here for everyone, whatever your story.

Desire	Haruki Murakami
Love	Jeanette Winterson
Marriage	Jane Austen
Babies	Anne Enright
Language	Xiaolu Guo
Motherhood	Helen Simpson
Fatherhood	Karl Ove Knausgaard
Family	Mark Haddon
Summer	Laurie Lee
Jealousy	Marcel Proust
Sisters	Louisa May Alcott
Home	Salman Rushdie
London	Charles Dickens
Race	Toni Morrison
Independence	Charlotte Brontë
Liberty	Virginia Woolf
Swimming	Roger Deakin
Friendship	Rose Tremain
Work	Joseph Heller
Money	Yuval Noah Harari
Austerity	Yanis Varoufakis
Injustice	Richard Wright

War	Sebastian Faulks
Murder	Arthur Conan Doyle
Depression	William Styron
Therapy	Stephen Grosz
Lies	Oscar Wilde
Drinking	John Cheever
Recovery	Helen Macdonald
Eating	Nigella Lawson
Parties	F. Scott Fitzgerald
Rave	Irvine Welsh
Psychedelics	Aldous Huxley
Art	Simon Schama
Calm	Tim Parks
Dreams	Sigmund Freud
Ghosts	M. R. James
Religion	Karen Armstrong
Science	Ian McEwan
Power	William Shakespeare
Freedom	Margaret Atwood
Death	Julian Barnes

vintageminis.co.uk